THE PLAINS

THE PLAINS
GERALD MURNANE

TEXT PUBLISHING
MELBOURNE AUSTRALIA

textpublishing.com.au

The Text Publishing Company
Swann House
22 William Street
Melbourne Victoria 3000
Australia

The Text Publishing Company (UK) Ltd
130 Wood Street
London, EC2V 6DL
United Kingdom

First published by Norstrilia Press 1982
Published by The Text Publishing Company 2000
This edition published 2017

Book design by W. H. Chong
Typeset by Midland Typesetters

Printed in Australia by Griffin Press, an Accredited ISO AS/NZS 14001:2004
Environmental Management System printer

National Library of Australia Cataloguing-in-Publication entry
ISBN: 9781925355901 (hardback)
ISBN: 9781925410266 (ebook)
Creator: Murnane, Gerald, 1939– author.
Title: The plains / by Gerald Murnane ; introduced by Ben Lerner.
Subjects: Families—Australia—Fiction. Plains—Australia—Fiction. Australia—
Social life and customs—Fiction.
Other Creators/Contributors: Lerner, Ben, 1979– writer of introduction.
Dewey Number: A823.3

CONTENTS

The Plain Sense of Things
by Ben Lerner

Having grown up in a small capital city located on the Great Plains of North America, I recognise something in Gerald Murnane's descriptions of expansive grasslands, unobstructed sky. He captures a plain's paradoxical mix of uniformity and mystery, the former producing the latter: small differences—a hill, a sudden patch of wildflowers—have an outsized power amid so much sameness; they'd fail to stand out among the dramatic natural beauties of California or the overwhelming built spaces of New York. Sometimes to break up long drives my dad would pull onto the shoulder of the highway and we would look for fossils in the limestone that crops out in the road cuts. The traces of ancient invertebrates with astonishing names (crinoids, fusulinids, and so on) were just one of many signs that the landscape my coastal relatives used to mock for its monotony in fact harboured wonders.

In Murnane's world, which both is and isn't Australia, the plain people and their plain speech also serve to conceal something—elaborate rituals, cosmologies, obscure passions, arcane knowledge. The apparent provincialism of the inhabitants of the plains is actually a kind of camouflage:

> A plainsman would not only claim to be ignorant of the ways of other regions but willingly appear to be misinformed about them. Most irritating of all to outsiders, he would affect to be without any distinguishing culture rather than allow his land and his ways to be judged part of some larger community of contagious tastes or fashions.

The cosmopolitan coasts leave nothing to the imagination. For Murnane, for the plainsmen, this obviously apparent richness of the actual is a kind of poverty. To quote the narrator of the short story 'Land Deal', a distant cousin of *The Plains*:

> Almost anything was possible. Any god might reside behind the thundercloud...The almost boundless scope of the possible was limited only by the occurrence of the actual. And it went without saying that what existed in the one sense could never exist in the other. Almost anything was possible except, of course, the actual.

The poet-philosophers of the plains (and every plainsman is one) know that the plains are unknowable in their totality, and are therefore charged with possibility. This is because what at first appears 'utterly flat and featureless' reveals, as you learn to look, 'countless subtle variations of landscape'. But it is also because there is another plain (or plains) behind this one, 'always invisible' even though you've 'crossed and recrossed it daily'. This is a book about the planes of the actual and the possible, about their interplay, how one haunts the other.

*

Murnane's sentences are little dialectics of boredom and beauty, flatness and depth. They combine a matter-of-factness, often approaching coldness, with an intricate lyricism; they are measured, both in the sense of 'restrained' and in the poetic sense of 'metrical', the former meaning often giving way to the second as you read. Take this sentence, although any of a thousand sentences would serve, from part two of *The Plains*: 'None of the scholars I mention can even guess how many successive encroachments of afternoon sunlight on the shadowy corners of libraries will have bleached the glossy inks on the books that they open at last.'

The sentence begins with an anthropological tone, the restricted affect of objectivity, but it transitions, starting with 'afternoon sunlight', into a more romantic register as it slowly zooms in on the letters and their lustre. The grammar here is both plain and elaborate: there is no internal punctuation, just a repetitive chain of prepositions (of, on, of, on), but there are delicate changes of light and shade and scale as the sentence unfolds. Beats fall with considerable regularity within the internal divisions of phrase and clause, so that a sense of poetic rhythm accumulates as you go. (I read it as anapaestic and dactylic—the accentual stresses tending to be divided by a pair of unstressed syllables.) Murnane's mysterious plainsmen pursue the 'lifelong task of shaping from uneventful days in a flat landscape the substance of myth'. And this is what Murnane achieves, again and again, through his carefully shaped sentences, the prosaic becoming poetic along their length.

*

The Plains is an ekphrastic novel, full of descriptions of other works of art. The narrator arrives from 'Outer Australia' ('the sterile margins of the continent'), as the people of the plains call it, determined to make the film—he plans to title it *The Interior*—that can capture the evasive truth of the plains. Much of his narrative is taken up with describing attempts in other media to produce artworks worthy of the place. There is the controversial painting *Decline and Fall of the*

Empire of Grass, for instance, which appears at first full of 'deliberately imprecise' shapes, 'of no style known from history', and yet, when you step back, you can see 'a painting of plants and soil'. There are poems, such as 'A Parasol at Noon', vaguely reminiscent of Wallace Stevens, which imagines 'a land apart' that is 'Neither a plain of old nor yet a dream'. And there is the composer who, in an attempt to find 'the musical equivalent of the characteristic sound of his district', stages a performance that, in Murnane's telling, sounds like a synthesis of Kafka and John Cage:

> the members of the orchestra were stationed far apart among the audience. Each instrument produced a volume of sound that could be heard only by the few listeners nearest it. The audience was free to move around—as quietly or as noisily as they wished. Some were able to hear snatches of melody as subtle as the scraping together of grass-blades or the throbbing of the brittle tissue of insects. A few even found some spot from which more than one instrument was audible. Most heard no music at all.

The works of art that Murnane describes are failures. The composer responds to critics of his work's insufficiency by saying that 'the purpose of his art was to draw attention to the impossibility of comprehending even such an obvious property of a plain as the sound that came from it.' And yet he hopes that he can capture a 'hint of the whole' through his experiments. For this composer, for Murnane, for his narrator, any serious art work will fail, as soon as it becomes actual, to capture the possible; but that failure itself can gesture toward, offer a hint of, the invisible topology that is no less real for being unrepresentable. A hint of the narrator's unmakeable film survives only by collapsing into this novel.

*

Gerald Murnane has never been on an aeroplane. He's left the state of Victoria few times in his almost eighty years. He suffers from anosmia, the inability to smell, although perhaps 'suffers' is the wrong word, as he says it has intensified his experience of colour, given him the gift of synaesthesia. ('If you were to say to me,' he told an interviewer, 'the smell of the lilac was very strong this afternoon, I would see little droplets of lilac-coloured moisture floating through the air.') To experience one sense in terms of another, to transpose smell onto the plane of vision, is a kind of embodied ekphrasis. Perhaps it adds to the mystery of the world to hear constant talk of a sense you don't possess, just as refusing to travel might keep the allure of other land-scapes intact.

Certainly Murnane is interested in what part of consciousness—of sensation, of emotion—might be shareable and what part is irreducibly individual, a private territory. This is a concern that scales up in his work from the question of what one person might know of another to larger questions of collectivity, of those 'imagined communities'—to borrow Benedict Anderson's famous phrase—called nations. While a plainsman likes 'to appear as a solitary inhabitant of a region that only he could explain', a nation of one, the plainsmen's constant debates about art, ornament, architecture, and archive, their rivalries and sports, their concern with differentiating themselves from Outer Australia, betray an obsession with constructing and contesting collective fictions. 'Australia' is the name of Murnane's supreme fiction, the idea that his private landscapes might somehow correspond with those of his countrymen and women, or at least be glimpsed by them, without having to be translated into mere 'taste or fashion', where commonality is purchased at the price of standardisation. *The Plains*, as much a prose poem as a novel, is this Australia's interior, Murnane's heartland, a realm of possibility, where 'the invisible is only what is too brightly lit.'

The Plains

'We had at length discovered a
country ready for the immediate
reception of civilised man...'

THOMAS LIVINGSTONE MITCHELL

*Three Expeditions into the
Interior of Eastern Australia*

{ one }

Twenty years ago, when I first arrived on the plains, I kept my eyes open. I looked for anything in the landscape that seemed to hint at some elaborate meaning behind appearances.

My journey to the plains was much less arduous than I afterwards described it. And I cannot even say that at a certain hour I knew I had left Australia. But I recall clearly a succession of days when the flat land around me seemed more and more a place that only I could interpret.

The plains that I crossed in those days were not endlessly alike. Sometimes I looked over a great shallow valley with scattered trees and idle cattle and perhaps a meagre stream at its centre. Sometimes, at the end of a tract of utterly unpromising country, the road rose towards what was unquestionably a hill before I saw ahead only another plain, level and bare and daunting.

In the large town that I reached on a certain afternoon, I noticed a way of speech and a style of dress that persuaded me I had come far enough. The people there were not quite the distinctive plainsmen I hoped to find in the remote central districts, but it suited me to know that ahead of me were more plains than I had yet crossed.

Late that night I stood at a third-storey window of the largest hotel in the town. I looked past the regular pattern of streetlights towards the dark country beyond. A breeze came in warm gusts from the north. I leaned into the surges of air that rose up from the nearest miles of grassland. I composed my face to register a variety of powerful emotions. And I whispered words that might have served a character in a film at the moment when he realised he had found where he belonged. Then I stepped back into the room and sat at the desk that had been specially installed for me.

I had unpacked my suitcases some hours earlier. Now my desk was stacked high with folders of note-paper and boxes of cards and an assortment of books with numbered tickets between their pages. On top of the stack was a medium-sized ledger labelled:

THE INTERIOR
(FILMSCRIPT)
MASTER KEY TO CATALOGUE OF
BACKGROUND NOTES
AND INSPIRATIONAL MATERIAL

I pulled out a bulky folder labelled *Occasional Thoughts—Not Yet in Catalogue* and wrote in it:

Not a soul in this district knows who I am or what I mean to do here. Odd to think that of all the plainsfolk lying asleep (in sprawling houses of white weatherboard with red iron roofs and great arid gardens dominated by pepper-trees and kurrajongs and rows of tamarisks) not one has seen the view of the plains that I am soon to disclose.

I spent the next day among the labyrinths of saloon bars and lounges on the ground floor of the hotel. All morning I sat alone in a deep leather armchair and stared at the strips of intolerable sunlight bordering the sealed venetian blinds in windows overlooking the main street. It was a cloudless day in early summer and the fierce morning sun reached even into the cavernous verandah of the hotel.

Sometimes I tilted my face slightly to catch the draught of cooler air from a fan overhead and watched the dew forming on my glass and thought with approval of the extremes of weather that afflicted the plains. Unchecked by hills or mountains, the sunlight in summer occupied the whole extent of the land from dawn till sunset. And in winter the winds and showers sweeping across the great open spaces barely faltered at the few stands of timber meant as shelter for men or animals. I knew there were great plains of the world that lay for months under snow, but I was pleased that my own district was not one of them. I much preferred to see all year the true configuration of the earth itself and not the false hillocks and hollows of some other element. In any case, I thought of snow (which I had never seen) as too much a part of European and American culture to be appropriate to my own region.

In the afternoon I joined one of the groups of plainsmen who strolled in from the main street and sat at their customary points along the enormous bars. I chose a group that seemed to include intellectuals and custodians of the history and lore of the district. I judged from their dress and bearing that they were not sheep-men or cattlemen, although they might have spent much of their time out of doors. A few had perhaps started life as the younger sons of the great landed families. (Everyone on the plains owed his prosperity to the land. Every town, large or small, was buoyed up by the bottomless wealth of the *latifundia* around it.) They all wore the dress of the cultivated, leisured class on the plains—plain grey trousers, rigidly creased, and spotless white shirt with matching tie-clip and armbands.

I was anxious to be accepted by these men and prepared for any test they might make of me. Yet I hardly
expected to call on anything I had read in my shelves
of books on the plains. To quote from works of literature would go against the spirit of the gathering,
although every man there would have read any book
that I named. Perhaps because they still felt themselves
encircled by Australia, the plainsmen preferred to think
of their reading as a private exercise that sustained them
in their public dealings but could not excuse them from
their obligation of cultivating an agreed tradition.

And yet, what was this tradition? Listening to the
plainsmen, I had a bewildering sense that they wanted
no common belief to fall back on: that each of them
became uncomfortable if another seemed to take as
understood something he himself claimed for the plains
as a whole. It was as though each plainsman chose to
appear as a solitary inhabitant of a region that only he
could explain. And even when a man spoke of his particular plain, he seemed to choose his words as though the
simplest of them came from no common stock but took

its meaning from the speaker's peculiar usage of it.

On that first afternoon I saw that what had sometimes been described as the arrogance of the plainsmen was no more than their reluctance to recognise any common ground between themselves and others. This was the very opposite (as the plainsmen themselves well knew) of the common urge among Australians of those days to emphasise whatever they seemed to share with other cultures. A plainsman would not only claim to be ignorant of the ways of other regions but willingly appear to be misinformed about them. Most irritating of all to outsiders, he would affect to be without any distinguishing culture rather than allow his land and his ways to be judged part of some larger community of contagious tastes or fashions.

*

I continued to keep to the hotel but almost every day I drank with a new group. For all my note-taking and drafting of plans and outlines, I was still far from sure of what my film would show. I expected to be granted some sudden strength of purpose from meeting a plainsman whose perfect assurance could only have come from his having just that day finished the last page of his notes for a novel or film to rival my own.

I had by then begun to speak freely in front of the plainsmen I met. A few wanted to hear my story before they divulged their own. I was prepared for this. I had been ready, if they only knew, to spend months of silent study in the libraries and art galleries of their town to prove I was no mere tourist or sightseer. But after a few days in the hotel I had devised a story that served me well.

I told the plainsmen that I was on a journey, which was true enough. I did not tell them the route I had followed to their town or the direction I might take when I left it. They would learn the truth when *The Interior* appeared as a film. In the meantime I let them believe I had begun my journey in a distant corner of the plains. And, as I had hoped, no one doubted me or even claimed to know the district I had named. The plains were so immense that no plainsman was ever surprised to hear of their encompassing some region he had never seen. Besides, many places far inland were subject to dispute—were they part of the plains or not? The true extent of the plains had never been agreed on.

I told them a story almost devoid of events or achievements. Outsiders would have made little of it, but the plainsmen understood. It was the kind of story that appealed to their own novelists and dramatists and poets. Readers and audiences on the plains were seldom impressed by outbursts of emotion or violent conflicts or sudden calamities. They supposed that the artists who presented such things had been beguiled by the noises of crowds or the profusions of shapes and surfaces in the foreshortened landscapes of the world beyond the plains. The plainsman's heroes, in life and in art, were such as the man who went home every afternoon for thirty years to an unexceptional house with neat lawns and listless shrubs and sat late into the night deciding on the route of a journey that he might have followed for thirty years only to arrive at the place where he sat—or the man who would never take even the one road that led away from his isolated farmhouse for fear that he would not recognise the place if he saw it from the distant vantage points that others used.

There were historians who suggested that the phenomenon of the plains themselves was responsible for the cultural differences between the plainsmen and Australians generally. The exploration of the plains had been the major event in their history. What had at first seemed utterly flat and featureless eventually disclosed countless subtle variations of landscape and an abundance of furtive wildlife. Trying to appreciate and describe their discoveries, the plainsmen had become unusually observant, discriminating, and receptive to gradual revelations of meaning. Later generations responded to life and art as their forebears had confronted the miles of grassland receding into haze. They saw the world itself as one more in an endless series of plains.

*

One afternoon I noticed a faint tension in the saloon bar that had become my favourite. Some of my companions kept their voices low. Others spoke with an uneasy stridence as though hoping to be overheard from a distant room. I realised that the day had come for me to test myself as a plainsman. Some of the great landowners had come to town, and a few of them were even then in the hotel.

I tried not to look agitated, and I watched my companions closely. Most of them too were anxious to be called into the distant inner lounge for a brief interview with the men they wanted for patrons. But my companions knew they might still be waiting at sundown or even at midnight. The estate owners on their infrequent visits cared nothing for the hours that townsmen observed. They liked to settle their commercial affairs in the early morning and then ensconce themselves in their favourite hotel lounges before lunchtime. They stayed there for as long as they pleased, drinking extravagantly and calling for snacks or entire meals at unpredictable intervals. Many stayed on until the morning or even the afternoon of the following day, with never more than one of the group dozing in his chair while the others talked privately or interviewed their petitioners from the town.

I followed the custom of sending in my name with one of the townsmen who happened to be called early. Then I learned what I could about the men in the remote lounge and wondered which of them would surrender a portion of his fortune and perhaps his own daughter in return for seeing his estates as the setting for the film that would reveal the plains to the world.

I drank sparingly all afternoon and checked my appearance in every mirror that caught my eye. My only cause for anxiety was the paisley-patterned silk cravat bunched in the open neck of my white shirt. By every rule of fashion that I knew, a cravat at a man's throat marked him out as wealthy, refined, sensitive, and possessed of ample leisure. But few plainsmen wore cravats, as I suddenly reminded myself. I could only hope the landowners would see in my dress the sort of paradox that discerning plainsmen delighted in. I wore

something that was part of the despised culture of the
capital cities—but only to distinguish myself a little
from my fellow-petitioners and to assert that the way
of the plains should be to avoid even the proper gesture
if it threatened to become merely fashionable.

Fingering my crimson paisley silk before the
mirror in the toilet, I was reassured by the sight of the
two dress rings on my left hand. Each was set with a
prominent slab of semi-precious stone—one a cloudy
blue-green and the other a subdued yellow. I could not
have named either stone, and the rings had been made
in Melbourne—the city I preferred to forget—but I had
chosen those colours for their special significance to
plainsmen.

I knew a little of the conflict between the
Horizonites and the Haremen, as they had come to be
called. I had bought my rings knowing that the colours
of the two factions were no longer worn in a spirit of
partisanship. But I had hoped to learn that one or the
other colour was sometimes preferred by plainsmen
who regretted the spiritedness of past disputes. When

I found that the practice was to wear never one colour alone but both, intertwined if possible, I had slipped the two rings onto separate fingers and never afterwards removed them.

I planned to represent myself to the landowners as a man from the very edge of the plains. They might comment on my wearing the two colours and ask me what traces of the famous dispute still survived in my remote homeland. If they did, I could tell them any of the stories I had heard of the lingering influence of the old quarrel. For I knew by then that the original issues survived in countless popular variants. Almost any opposite viewpoints that arose in public or private debate might be labelled the Horizonites' or the Haremen's. Almost any duality that occurred to a plainsman seemed easier to grasp if the two entities were associated with the two hues, blue-green and faded gold. And everyone on the plains remembered from childhood the day-long games of Hairies and Horrors— the frantic pursuits far into the paddocks, or the insecure hiding-places in the long grass.

If the landowners wanted to talk at length with me about 'the colours' (the modern name for all the complex rivalries of the past century), there was nothing to prevent me from offering them my own erratic interpretation of the celebrated conflict. By late afternoon I was no longer so eager to show them how close I was to their own ways of thinking. It seemed just as important to give them evidence of my imaginative prowess.

And then the door from the street was flung open and a new group of plainsmen came in from the dazzling sunlight with their afternoon's work done and settled themselves at the bar to resume their lifelong task of shaping from uneventful days in a flat landscape the substance of myth. I felt a sudden elation at not knowing what could be verified in the history of the plains or even in my own history. And I even began to wonder whether the landowners might prefer me to appear before them as a man who misunderstood the plains.

*

Waiting all that day in my saloon bar, I came to learn of the capriciousness of the landowners. A townsman had gone in to them with bundles of designs and samples for a series of handprinted volumes. He wanted to publish for the first time some of the many manuscript diaries and collections of letters still preserved in the great houses. Some of the landowners had seemed interested. But in answering their questions the man had been too cautious and conciliatory. He had assured them that his editor would seek their advice before including any material likely to cause scandal. This was not what the great men wanted to hear. They feared no harm from their families' follies being known all over the plains. When the publisher had first begun to speak, each of them had seen the whole mass of his family archives being issued year after year in costly bindings embossed with his own insignia. The projector's talk of suppressions, of abridgements, had suddenly checked the steady expansion of their collected papers along imagined shelves. Or so the man himself had surmised afterwards when he talked with me of his failure. He had quietly put away his mock-ups and samples of paper and typefaces and left the room while the landowners were trying to calculate, by no means frivolously, how many individual lifetimes might be required to assemble, to read and comprehend, and then to decide on the significance of the lifetime of a man who delighted (as each of them certainly did) in filling drawers and chests and filing cabinets with every document, even the briefest scribbled note, that hinted at the vast unseen zone where he spent most of his days and nights.

But one of the townsmen who followed the publisher into the inner lounge had come back whispering that his future was assured. He was a young man previously unable to earn a living from his specialised interests. He had studied the history of furnishings, fabrics and interior design in the great homes of the plains. Most of his research had been done in museums and libraries, but he had recently arrived at a theory that he could test only by visiting some mansion where the tastes and preferences of several generations were all evident under the one roof. I understood the main claim of the theory to be that the first generation of land-owners on the plains had been fond of complex designs and profusely ornamented objects that seemed to contrast with the simplicity and bareness of the land-scapes around their homes, whereas later generations chose to decorate more simply as the plains outside became marked by roads and fences and plantations. But this principle was always modified in its operation by two others: first, that in the early days a house was furnished more elaborately the nearer it was situated to the supposed centre of the plains or, in other words, the further it was from the coastal birthplaces of the first plainsmen, whereas in more recent times the reverse applied, that is, the homes nearer the putative centre, and once thought remote, were now considered close to some ideal source of cultural influence and decorated with less zest, while those nearer the margin of the plains were fitted out in great detail as though to compensate for a bleakness that their owners perceived not far off, in the lands beyond the plains.

The young man explained his theory to the landowners soon after midnight. He had proposed it hesitantly and reminded them that it could only be verified after months of research in great homes of every district of the plains. But the landowners were delighted with it. One of them took the floor and announced that the theory might justify a suspicion he had whenever he walked alone late at night through the longest galleries and across some of the vast halls of his mansion. At such times he felt obscurely that the appearance and the exact position of every painting and statue and chest and the arrangement of collections of silverware and porcelain and even of the butterflies and shells and pressed flowers under their dusty glass had been determined by forces of great moment. He saw the countless objects in his home as a few visible points on some invisible graph of stupendous complexity. If his impression was unusually powerful he peered at the repeated motifs in a tapestry as though to read the story of a certain succession of days or years long before his time, or he stared at the intricate brilliance of a chandelier and guessed at the presence of sunlight in the memories of people he himself scarcely remembered.

The same landowner began to describe other influences that he felt late at night in the more remote wings of his house. He sensed sometimes the lingering persistence of forces that had failed—of a history that had almost come into being. He found himself looking into corners for the favourite pieces of the unborn children of marriages that were never made.

But his companions shouted him down. This was not what the young man, their astute historian of culture, had in mind. They listened while a second speaker proposed a method for allotting a numerical value to each of the influences described by the young man, then correcting (by what the speaker called 'some sort of sliding scale') the dominance of prosperous years over lean times, and finally devising a formula that would 'come up with' (his own words again) the true, essential style of the plains—the golden mean of all the variations that had occurred in different places and times.

While this man had been talking, another had sent

for sheets of graph paper and a box of finely sharpened coloured pencils. He replied to the latest speaker that his golden mean was no more than a grey average and that the great value of the young man's theory was not that it could be used to calculate any one traditional style but that it allowed each family to plot its own graph, showing all the co-ordinates of culture that made its own style unique. And he cleared a table and called the young man to help him with his graph.

The next hours, so the young man told me afterwards, were the most rewarding of his life. All but one of the landowners sent for supplies of paper and pencils and sat down among the ashtrays and glasses and empty bottles to plot the coloured lines that might reveal unguessed-at harmonies beneath the seeming confusion of a century and a half of impulsiveness and eccentricity. They soon agreed that each colour should denote the same cultural vector in each of their charts. And they referred all doubtful points to the young man for his ruling. But even so, the variety of patterns that appeared was remarkable. As time passed, some men left off their calculations and began to compose simpler, stylised versions of their designs or to reduce outstanding features to motifs for emblems. They had all been remarking for some time on a gradual change in the intensity of their colours before someone stepped into a hallway and came back to announce that a cloudless dawn was breaking over the plains.

The men put down their pencils and served themselves a new round of drinks and made reckless offers of fees to the young man for his services as a consultant historian of fashion. But he begged to tell them that while they had been busy over their charts, the one man who had hung back had appointed him as resident historian of design and adviser on matters of taste in his own household—with lifetime tenure, an absurdly generous stipend, and an annual allowance for private research and travel.

This particular landowner had not been so interested in plotting the influences on his family's taste in past years. He had suddenly seen the possibility of employing the young man to isolate and quantify every received idea and respected theory of the present day, every tradition and preference that survived from the past, and every prediction of future changes in the value of current beliefs; to give due weight to family legends and local customs and whatever else distinguished one household from all others; to allow for the limited exercise of whim and caprice in the choices of the present generation; and so to arrive at a formula that he, the landowner, and his family could use to decide which of any number of paintings or furnishings or colour schemes or table settings or bindings of books or topiary work or outfits of clothing was most likely to establish such a standard of elegance that other families would have to include it as a constant in their own formulae of fashion.

The young man finished his story and went home to sober up. I ate a hasty breakfast and went on thinking of the Horizonites and Haremen. The success of the young designer had encouraged me to be bold with the landowners. When it appeared unlikely that I would be called in to them before lunch, I adjusted the hand that encircled my glass and stared at the two stones on my fingers. An electric globe was still burning on the wall just behind me. The light was refracted through my beer (the darkest of the nine varieties brewed on the plains) into a diffuse aura that seemed to quench the more intense hues of each gem. Their essential colours persisted but the contrast between them had been lessened by the glow from the ale.

It occurred to me to present myself to the land-owners as a man destined to reconcile in my own life or, better still, in my film, all the conflicting themes arising from the old quarrel between the blue-greens and the old-golds. As if to encourage my enterprise, a loud but not undignified roar sounded just then from the distant room where the great men were beginning the second day of their session.

*

I had heard that at one stage of the dispute, bands of men were armed and drilled in the back paddocks of certain estates. And yet the whole matter had begun with a cautiously expressed manifesto signed by an obscure group of poets and painters. I did not even know the year of this manifesto—only that it fell during a decade when the artists of the plains were finally refusing to allow the word 'Australian' to be applied to themselves or their work. Those were the years when plainsmen generally began to use the term 'Outer Australia' for the sterile margins of the continent. But if it was a period of excitement it was also the age when plainsmen acknowledged that their distinctive forms of expression were for themselves alone. For all that outsiders would know of them, the poets and musicians and painters of the plains might never have existed and no peculiar culture have survived within the drab outer layers of Australia.

One small group in those days formed around a certain poet whose first published volume was a collection named for its most arresting poem, 'The Horizon, After All'. The poetry itself was never labelled as derivative, but the poet and his group offended many by gathering regularly in a bar that served a sort of wine (most plainsmen had a congenital dislike for this drink) and discussing aesthetics much too loudly. They identified themselves by the wearing of a blue and a green ribbon, fastened so as to overlap. Later, after much searching, they found a cloth dyed an unusual blue-green, from which they cut single ribbons of the famous 'tint of the horizon'.

What this group originally proposed had been almost lost among the jumble of doctrines and precepts and so-called philosophies later attributed to them. They may well have intended no more than to provoke the intellectuals of the plains to define in metaphysical terms what had previously been expressed in emotional or sentimental language. (This seemed to me the best summary of the matter that I had heard, even though I had always had the greatest difficulty in understanding what metaphysics were.) It was clear that they felt for the plains the passionate love that artists and poets had so often professed. But people who read their poems or inspected their paintings found few renderings of actual places on the plains. The group seemed to be insisting that what moved them more than wide grasslands and huge skies was the scant layer of haze where land and sky merged in the farthest distance.

Members of the group were challenged, of course, to explain themselves. They replied by talking of the blue-green haze as though it was itself a land—a plain of the future, perhaps, where one might live a life that existed only in potentiality on the plains where poets and painters could do no more than write or paint. The critics then accused the group of rejecting the actual plains for a landscape that was wholly illusory. But the group argued that the zone of haze was as much a part of the plains as any configuration of soil or clouds. They said they esteemed the land of their birth for the very reason that it seemed bounded continually by the blue-green veil that urged them to dream of a different plain. Most critics dismissed such statements as wilfully evasive and chose to ignore the group from then on.

But the controversy was kept alive by the appearance soon afterwards of another group of artists who seemed equally keen to provoke criticism. This group exhibited a roomful of paintings with a novel subject-matter. The most impressive of many similar works, *Decline and Fall of the Empire of Grass*, seemed at first sight only a very detailed study of a small patch of native grasses and herbage—a few square yards from any one of the countless grazing paddocks on the plains. But spectators soon began to make out of the trampled stems and frayed foliage and minute, severed blossoms the shapes of things quite unconnected with the plains.

Many of the shapes seemed deliberately imprecise, and even those that most nearly represented architectural ruins or abandoned artifacts were of no style known from history. But commentators could point to a score of details that seemed to comprise a scene of grandiose desolation—and then, stepping back, could see once again a painting of plants and soil. The artist himself encouraged the search for shattered colonnades and tapestries flapping on roofless walls. But in his only published account of the painting (a brief statement which he tried repeatedly to amend in later years) he claimed it was inspired by his study of a certain small marsupial. This animal had disappeared from settled areas before the plainsfolk had given a common name to it. The artist used its unwieldy scientific name, but someone in the course of debate referred to it (inaccurately) as a plains-hare, and that name stuck.

The painter had studied a few passages in the journals of explorers and early naturalists and a single stuffed skin in a plains museum. Observers had remarked on the animal's attempts to hide by flattening itself in the grass. The early settlers had walked boldly up and clubbed hundreds of the creatures to death for their barely usable hides. Rather than flee, the animal seemed to trust to the last in its colouring—the same dull gold that predominated in the grass of the plains.

The painter, so he said, found a large significance in the stubborn foolishness of this almost-forgotten species. All its near-relatives were burrowing animals. It might have used its powerful claws for digging the spacious, well-concealed tunnels that kept other species safe. But it was obliged to cling for safety to its barren surroundings; to persist in seeing the shallow grass of the plains as a fortress against intruders.

The man who made these claims insisted that he was no mere nature lover calling for the return of vanished wildlife. He wanted the people of the plains to see their landscape with other eyes; to recover the promise, the mystery even, of the plains as they might have appeared to someone with no other refuge. He and his fellow artists would assist them. His group utterly rejected the supposed appeal of misty distances. They were pledged to find grand themes in the weathered gold of their birthplace.

None of this was any better received than the earlier manifesto in favour of an 'art of the horizon'. The earliest attacks on the painters accused them of wilfully inventing subjects unconnected with the essential spirit of the plains. Other critics predicted that the end of the painters as a group would be as swift as that of the pathetic animal that so inspired them. But the painters took to wearing their dull-gold ribbons and debating with the men of the blue-green group.

The dispute might have been soon forgotten by all but the rival groups. But it was transformed once more into an issue of wider interest when a third group tried to promote its own views at the expense of the blue-greens' and the old-golds'. This third group concocted a theory of art so eccentric that it angered the most tolerant of plainsmen. Even laymen, writing in the daily press, saw the theory as a threat to the precious fabric of culture on the plains. And the blue-greens and old-golds set aside their differences and joined with their former critics and with artists and writers of every sort in condemning the new absurdity.

They discredited it finally on the simple grounds that it was derived from ideas current in Outer Australia. The plainsmen were not always opposed to borrowings and importations, but in the matter of culture they had come to scorn the seeming barbarisms of their neighbours in the coastal cities and damp ranges. And when the more acute plainsmen had convinced the public that this latest group were drawing on a jumble of the worst kinds of foreign notions, the members of the despised group chose to cross the Great Dividing Range rather than endure the enmity of all thinking plainsmen.

Then, because the discredited group had originally used their theory to attack both the blue-greens and the old-golds, these two factions enjoyed for a while a large share of the general goodwill towards artists. For, as one commentator reminded the public (in the inflated prose of that era), 'Their notions may be no more acceptable to us now than before. But we recognise them as fundamentally inspired by our incomparable landscape and, therefore, as connected, however tenuously, with the great body of our cherished mythology. And what they propose seems entirely reasonable beside the preposterous fallacy that we have lately banished from our plains: the specious argument for the artist's concerning himself with the distribution of material wealth or the workings of Government or the release of men from the constraints of morality in the name of a universal licence masking itself as Freedom.'

But, as I knew from my research among borrowed books and my long conversations in saloon bars, the public had soon tired of quarrels among artists. For many years the two inimical theories were of interest to no one but a few diehards hunched over acrid wines in back bars or haranguing casual acquaintances at opening nights in inferior art galleries.

Yet in the years that some liked to call the Second Great Age of Exploration, two groups arose who were proud to be called Horizonites and Haremen. And the two colours reappeared—not merely in buttonholes but on gaudy silk banners at the head of public processions and in hand-lettered pennants over gateposts. The disputes of those days had little to do with poetry or painting. The self-proclaimed Horizonites claimed to be men of action. They called themselves the true plainsmen, ready to push back the limits of pasturage into regions too long neglected. The Haremen insisted that *they* were the practical ones, and contrasted their own realistic plans for closer settlement with their opponents' grand schemes for populating a desert.

•   Thirty years later again the colours were mostly
seen on the tiny enamelled pins worn discreetly by
estate agents and owners of small businesses. These
were the badges of the two major parties in local
government. Blue-green denoted the Progressive
Mercantile Party, with its policy of establishing new
industries and building railway lines between the plains
and the capital cities. Gold was the colour of the Plains
First League, whose slogan was 'Buy Local Goods'.

    The great landowners of those days mostly kept
aloof from politics. Yet it was observed that at the end
of every polo season, when two combined sides were
chosen from the dozens of smaller associations and
leagues, the team calling themselves Central Plains
always wore a certain shade of yellow when they rode
out against the men representing the Outer Plains. In
the official program the Outer Plains uniform was
described as 'sea-green' but the sea was five hundred
miles away.

    I had listened to men who had stood as small boys
in the crowds watching those polo games. Some of

them, looking back, remembered odd words that proved their fathers knew what was in the air. But my informants were sure that as boys they had seen nothing ominous in the hectic clash of colours. A blue-green might break loose and dash alone towards the far goal. A knot of golds might pursue him, gaining steadily, the very tilt of their bodies—low over the flapping manes— suggesting menace. But it still seemed no more than sport—the traditional game of the plains, whose technical terms made up so many figures of speech in the plainsmen's dialect.

They knew now, so they had told me, that those years had been an interval of halcyon weather on the plains. The dual colours of the horsemen hinted every moment at some pattern about to appear out of the dusty field. High overhead the countless clouds of the plains formed vast but equally unstable patterns of their own. The dense crowd stood mostly silent (as crowds will on the plains, where the empty air brings back few echoes and where even the loudest cry may be followed by a sudden and disturbing quietness). And the children saw what they should have remembered afterwards as no more than well-meant rivalry between teams of the finest horsemen of the plains.

The plainsmen still resented the term 'secret society', but it seemed to me the only possible name for either of the two mysterious movements that had spread for years through the networks of polo clubs and probably, too, among the jockey clubs and athletic leagues and associations of riflemen. No leaders had ever been identified. The horsemen and sharpshooters who exercised in lonely corners of remote estates saw only their immediate commanders. Even the councils that met in panelled drawing rooms beneath silken flags (of novel designs but always with one of two well-known colours prominent) were apparently conducted with no show of deference towards any of the three or four who had secretly elected a leader from their own number.

Almost certainly both societies had begun with the same general aim—to promote whatever distinguished the plains from the rest of Australia. And it must have been many years before either society considered the extreme proposal of absolute political independence for the plains. But inevitably the more daring of the theorists in each group gained influence. The Brotherhood of the Endless Plain devoted themselves to an elaborate scheme for transforming Australia into a Union of States whose seat of government was far inland and whose culture welled up from its plains and spilled outwards. The coastal districts would then be seen as a mere borderland where truly Australian customs were debased by contact with the Old World. The League of Heartlanders wanted nothing less than a separate Republic of the Plains with manned frontier-posts on every road and railway line that crossed the Great Dividing Range.

I had always supposed that plainsmen must regard armed revolt as somehow demeaning. And when I first learned the history of the plains I doubted the stories of private armies masquerading as polo clubs. My friends in the saloon bars could offer me little evidence. But in any case, the tale they told did not end in pitched battles. In the humid air of a certain summer men began muttering that the time had come. It was a season of exceptional storms, so that even the spacious land seemed constricted by a nameless tension. And then word came that the plains had settled for peace.

No one who passed on the message knew in which library or smoking-room of which mansion the decision had been taken. But those who heard the news realised that somewhere out on one of the oldest estates some great plainsman had lost sight of a particular vision of the plains. They heard the news and went back to their quiet routines and perhaps noticed in the air the glassy clarity of the approaching autumn.

For some years afterwards there were savage brawls after the great annual polo matches. A man who had seen his father lose an eye one Saturday afternoon told me years later that this was the only fighting the plainsmen had ever been capable of. There had never been any likelihood, he told me, of armies from the plains marching under banners of the blue-green or the gold against outsiders. Some landowner, isolated in his book-lined rooms behind leafy verandahs and acres of lawns at the heart of his miles of silent land, had been dreaming of a plain that ought to have been. He had talked to others of his kind. All the trappings of the secret societies, the privately printed essays reviving forgotten quarrels, the whispered plans for military campaigns—all these had been the work of lonely, deluded men. They had talked of separating the plains from Australia when they themselves were already marooned on their great grassy islands impossibly far from the mainland.

The son of the brawler told me that in all the battles behind sports pavilions and on hotel verandahs the colours ripped from men's coats or clenched in bloodied fists had signified only the two sporting associations of 'Central' and 'Outer'. He claimed to know nothing of a story that I had heard elsewhere of a third group disrupting the great annual matches and throwing themselves into the thickest of the fighting until the blue-greens and the golds were sometimes forced to unite against them. Yet I knew that a few local associations had later combined briefly to choose a team with the name Inner Australia and uniforms red for the sunrise or the sunset or, perhaps, something unstated.

I wondered how much these obscure sportsmen might have known of the dissident group that had once been expelled from the Brotherhood of the Endless Plain. The Inner Australians had apparently disappeared even more swiftly than the two older societies. But at least they had been discussed occasionally in historical journals. Like the Brotherhood from which they seceded, the Inner Australians proposed that the whole continent known as Australia should be one nation with one culture. And they insisted, of course, that the culture should be that of the plains rather than the spurious ways of the coast. But whereas the Brotherhood envisaged an Australian Government dominated by plainsmen with a policy of transforming the continent into one gigantic plain, the Inner Australians refused to talk of political power, which they claimed was wholly illusory.

In fact, the Inner Australians had been divided

amongst themselves. The best-remembered of them
argued for a hasty military adventure. They hoped not
for success but for a memorable failure against much
superior numbers. They resolved to conduct themselves, after their capture, as citizens of a real nation
who happened to be detained by the forces of an anti-
nation compounded of the negatives of all the attributes
of Inner Australia.

A minority (some said two or three only) argued
that the plains would never receive their due until the
continent then known as Australia was renamed Inner
Australia. No other change need be made to the
appearance or condition of what had formerly been
Australia. The coast-dwellers would soon discover what
the plainsmen had always known—that talk of a nation
presupposed the existence of certain influential but
rarely seen landscapes deep within the territory
referred to.

And then, so it was said, not long before the
sudden collapse of the secret societies one man had
dissociated himself from the minority of Inner

Australians and had taken up the most extreme of all positions. He denied the existence of any nation with the name Australia. There was, he admitted, a certain legal fiction which plainsmen were sometimes required to observe. But the boundaries of true nations were fixed in the souls of men. And according to the projections of real, that is spiritual, geography, the plains clearly did not coincide with any pretended land of Australia. Plainsmen were therefore free to obey any parliament of State or Commonwealth (as, of course, they had always done) and even to participate in the New State Movement, which the secret societies had previously condemned as a farce. It was expedient for plainsmen to appear as citizens of the nonexistent nation. The alternative was to upset a neatly poised complex of delusions and to have the borders of the plains beset by a horde of exiles from the nation that had never been.

*

Towards lunchtime in the almost empty bar, I tried to recall the notes I had made some days before from a scholarly article in one of the three fortnightly journals of criticism and comment published on the plains. The notes were in my room upstairs but I could not leave the bar—the landowners might have called for me at any moment. (I had not found time even to shave or wash, but petitioners who obtained an audience on the second day were always careful to look haggard and dishevelled. The landowners liked to think that while they themselves coped easily with a night of drinking, their clients were of feebler constitution.)

The author of the article had seemed to claim that all the disputes between factions on the plains were symptoms of a basic polarity in the temperament of the plainsman. Anyone surrounded from childhood by an abundance of level land must dream alternately of exploring two landscapes—one continually visible but never accessible and the other always invisible even though one crossed and recrossed it daily.

What I could not remember was the theory arrived

at in the dense final paragraphs of the article. The author had postulated the existence of a landscape where a plainsman might finally resolve the contradictory impulses that his native land gave rise to. After lunch, when I was drinking steadily again and things around me had regained their vibrancy, I succeeded in recalling a note I had made in the margin of the scholar's article: 'I, a film-maker, am admirably equipped to explore this landscape and reveal it to others.'

*

By late afternoon I had watched perhaps twenty clients going singly into the inner room and coming out again. And I had noticed that the largest groups among them were the designers of emblems and the founders of religions.

Before their interviews the men of both these groups were invariably tense and anxious and careful not to let slip any details of their projects to rivals. As

time passed it became apparent that few of these clients
succeeded in the inner room. The landowners were
known for their obsession with emblems and forms of
heraldic art peculiar to the plains. And although religion
was rarely discussed on the plains, I knew that it too
had its passionate devotees in almost every great house.
But the clients who specialised in these subjects were
competing against experts already in favour with the
landowners.

No great house could have done without its
resident advisers on emblematic art. Most families made
all their new appointments from among the sons and
nephews of their senior staff, believing that their traditions were only safe in the hands of men who had
been exposed to them since childhood. Even when an
outsider was appointed, he was expected to have spent
some years acquiring at his own expense a detailed
knowledge of genealogy, family history and legends,
and those preferences and inclinations that were only
revealed in close conversations late at night, hasty
entries in diaries on bedside tables, sketches of paintings

pinned behind doors, manuscript poems torn to pieces in the last hours before dawn. When a post was vacant it was not unknown for a footman of the household or a tutor from the schoolroom to announce that his years of menial service had only been undertaken to qualify him as a creator of heraldic art. Then the members of the family knew the reason for the uncommon alertness they had often noticed about the man, his untoward appearance in certain rooms at inappropriate times, his formal requests to spend his scant leisure time in the library, his being seen in the furthest paddocks collecting rare plants or discovered afterwards in his quarters peering at the shapes of leaves through a reading glass that someone had missed weeks earlier from a private drawer. But a talented designer was valued so highly that if the man proved his competence he was appointed to the post he coveted and only praised for his enterprise during all those years of furtive study.

The great houses exhibited their emblems and crests and liveries and racing colours at every opportunity. Families who for generations had scorned all display of wealth or influence would draw a visitor's attention to a certain design on silverware and table napery or the choice of colours on the painted wood-work of outdoor aviaries or conservatories. I had read a little of the mass of scholarly commentaries on a concern that had reached an extreme of refinement among plainsfolk. And I remembered an essay by a neglected philosopher who contributed for his liveli-hood to the Saturday pages of a declining newspaper.

This writer had argued that each man in his heart is a traveller in a boundless landscape. But even the plainsmen (who should have learned not to fear hugeness of horizons) looked for landmarks and signposts in the disquieting terrain of the spirit. A plainsman who was compelled to multiply the appear-ances of his monogram or some novel choice of colours in the visible plains was only marking the limits of the territory that he recognised. Such a man would have done better to explore whatever was beyond the illusions that could be signified by simple shapes and motifs.

This account was disputed by other theorists who claimed that a concern for emblems was just the sort of exploration that the philosopher had called for. Thus, when a man displayed his colours on the bindings in his library, he asserted, perhaps a trifle crudely, that no end was yet in sight to the regions he knew in his heart.

The landowners themselves took no part in the learned discussions of their pursuit. This was not because they lacked a taste for intellectual endeavour but because the actual practice of heraldic art could offer sufficient scope for the most active mind. Many a landowner joined with the designers he had commissioned in their exacting task of finding some theme underlying the history of his family, some motif suggested by the geological structure of his estates, or some ideograph of a species of plant or animal peculiar to his district.

And while all these tasks went forward in the great houses, the many unemployed students and scholars of the subject added to their knowledge or perfected their skills in public libraries and museums and rented studios and among the outlying swamps and plantations of estates whose vastness and complexity they dreamed of reducing to a stylised image on a simple field.

Some of those who waited on the great land-owners in their hotel bar explained to me that their best hope was to convince a particular landowner that his family's heraldic art derived from too narrow a range of disciplines. One petitioner intended to outline the results of his research into entomology and to argue that the metallic hues and the prolonged rituals of a certain wasp with a restricted habitat might correspond to something that had not yet been expressed in the art of the family whose patronage he courted. Another petitioner meant to offer his findings from years of study in meteorology, confident that a certain landowner could not fail to see the relevance for him of the vagaries of a seasonal wind when it approached his lands.

There were others who approached the land-owners with nothing to recommend them but their programs for displaying more widely whatever colours and devices were already established in a family. I heard of a scheme for building a system of indoor aquaria and stocking each tank with fish of one species only but arranging the whole so that viewers might see, through numerous thicknesses of pellucid glass and intervals of faintly clouded water and images of clouded water in faintly clouded glass, multiform patterns of two colours that mattered. One man had perfected a process for working the most vivid of dyes into the finest of saddlery. Another spoke guardedly of a theatre, predictably decorated, but with tableaux of marionettes to mimic even those characters commemorated by a mere stem of foliage or a stripe of colour in a familiar coat of arms.

The most secretive of the waiting men could have been of service only to a landowner who was himself a lover of secrecy. There were a few such heads of families who laboured over their emblems for years but then concealed them partly or wholly. They might speak proudly of them to a few friends, but theirs was the solitary appreciation of a soothing harmony or an arresting contrast that only they could be fully aware of. A petitioner in search of such men carried a stock of panes and lenses, mysteriously tinted, for altering or effacing certain colours; pigments sensitive to the least sunlight; canvases and panellings and bolts of silk all with double thicknesses.

All these groups had some justification for approaching even a landowner known to have settled long before on the patterns and colours that stood for all he valued. But there were also a few petitioners with only a broad knowledge of their subject. These politely offered their services to the assembled landowners in the hope that one great house might just then have declared its heraldic art 'veiled'.

The word had come to be used only figuratively in my day, but in earlier times a carriage would be seen with a small train of black or purple velvet draped across each painted panel. And when the coachman, ill at ease in his makeshift grey, steered the horses around the sweeping driveway at evening, certain windows only mirrored the uniform colour of the sky, the same dark velvet having been hung behind them for the sake of some small coloured pane.

Itinerant designers sometimes got wind of a veiling when they observed a vague irritation and discontent among members of a great family or heard of long conferences in locked libraries and of servants afterwards working until midnight to put away books and manuscripts previously untouched for years. But most veilings were announced with so little warning that even a designer attached to the household would be taken by surprise (and obliged without notice to question the value of his life's work).

Sometimes no public announcement was made—more from a passing impatience with formality than from any desire to conceal the event. But a caller at a remote mansion could see the evidence at once. The flagpoles stood bare above the tennis courts. Painters worked at the pavilions by the polo fields. Workmen on many-storeyed scaffolding prised fragments of glass from leaded windows and, for all the urgency of their task, paused to look out on some quarter of the plains through the formless chip of colour that might once have completed a symbol of fame. Indoors, french polishers stepped among heaps of tangled threads left by the seamstresses as they picked out from tapestries all traces of a device that had once seemed part of the very fabric. And in some far, quiet room, the gold-smiths, with eyes made monstrous by lenses gripped under their brows, unclasped from heirlooms the jewels whose settings had been declared unworthy of them.

This was the slight hope that urged the least-prepared of the petitioners into the inner room of the hotel—that some landowner there might be just then in the grip of the mild madness that could only end when all he owned was stamped or carved or embroi-dered or painted with proof that he had interpreted his life afresh.

I had learned this much from the students of emblems. But I knew better than to question the founders of religions. I had never heard a plainsman talk seriously of his religious beliefs. Like the

Australians on the distant coast, the plainsmen often commended religion in general as a force for good. And, as on the coast, there was still a minority of families who sat through Sunday services, Catholic or Protestant, in the drab parish churches or the cathedrals with their incongruous European aspects. But I knew that these observances and the commonplace sentiments uttered in public were often meant to draw attention away from the true religions of the plains.

These flourished in their purest forms among families who had long abandoned the traditional churches (and with them folk memories from the late Roman Empire or Elizabethan England) and spent their Sundays in seeming idleness among the silent rooms of their isolated mansions. I had heard of no sect numbering more than three or four and none whose tenets could be codified or even paraphrased by the most eloquent of its followers. I was assured that elaborate rituals were practised and their efficacy extolled. Yet it seemed that men who had watched the sectaries day after day, and even spied on them in their most private moments, had seen nothing that any irreligious plainsman might not have done—and thought ordinary or even trivial.

There was this same mystery about the group who waited with me in the hotel—the so-called founders of religions. There was a certain impressiveness about them, but nothing they said or did might have explained why they were so often welcomed into the great houses. (I had heard that few of them secured permanent employment. They practised for brief periods, at lucrative rates, after which they fell from favour and were dismissed, or they declared their tasks fulfilled and resigned.) And a man of a different profession who had happened to observe one of them courting the favour of a group of landowners had seen the priest of obscure persuasion only urging the great men to drink and talk while he listened.

At one time I had begun to doubt the existence of these esoteric creeds of the plains. But then certain plainsmen had been pointed out to me. I can only explain the impression they made on me by saying that they seemed to know what most men only guess at. Somewhere out among the swaying grasses of their estates, or in the least-visited rooms of their rambling homesteads, they had learned the true stories of their lives and known the men they might have been.

Whenever it had occurred to me to envy the plainsmen who drew such strength from their private religions, I had gone upstairs to my hotel room and gravely sat down and added to the notes for my film-script as though that was part of my own religious quest that some stranger wondered about.

*

I was called into the inner room at the very hour when the authority and prodigality of the great landowners seemed most awesome. In one of the passageways leading to their bar I glanced over my shoulder at a distant door. The transom window above it was a minute rectangle of intense light—a signal that the plains outside languished under mid-afternoon. But it was an afternoon that the landowners knew nothing of. No tale that I had heard of their wealth impressed me so much as their careless dismissal of a whole day. I walked into their smoky room still half-blinded by the fragment I had glimpsed of the sunlight they spurned.

My only shock came from the sight of the stretcher in the corner. They were not all, perhaps, the giants of legend. One man lay motionless on the bare canvas. But only a hand pressed awkwardly against his eyes suggested that his sleep was not untroubled. The others sat erect on stools at the bar. One of them poured nearly half a jug of beer into a pewter pot engraved with a strange monogram and handed it to me. Someone else pushed a stool towards me with his foot. But it was half an hour before anyone spoke to me.

There were six of them at the bar, all in suits of the discreetly patterned fabric that I called 'tweed'. A few had loosened their ties or undone a top button on their shirts, and one man's shoes (massive all-leather soles and ox-blood uppers with elaborate whorls and arcs of dots punched from them) were conspicuously unlaced. But every man had still a sureness and elegance that made me finger my own cravat and twist the rings on my fingers.

I thought at first that they were talking only of women. But then I distinguished three quite separate conversations, each advancing steadily. Sometimes one or other topic occupied them all, but usually each man divided his attention among the three debates, leaning across the man beside him or leaving his stool for a moment to engage some opponent along the bar. And there were long intervals when they all enjoyed some joke that I found irrelevant or puzzling. They were all in a condition that I expected to reach myself after a few more pots of beer. They had lost little of their customary dignity. Perhaps they spoke a trifle too emphatically or gestured too readily. As I understood it from my own experiences with alcohol, they had drunk themselves sober.

In that condition, as I knew it, they were able to discover a startling significance in almost every object or fact. They were compelled to repeat certain statements for the ring of profundity they seemed to give off. Each man's history acquired the unity of a great work of art, so that when he recounted something from his past, he dwelt on the least details for the meaning they derived from the whole. Above all, they saw that the future was well in hand. They need only remember afterwards the insights just granted them. And if even those were not enough, they could foresee another morning when they walked inside from the sunlight and began to drink seriously and steadily until all the baffling brightness of the world was only a glowing horizon at the far edge of their deep private twilight.

The landowners went on talking. After my second pot was emptied I was ready to join them. But they were in no hurry to interview me. I was careful not to show impatience. I wanted to prove that I was already attuned to their ways; that I was prepared to put aside all else and devote an hour or a day to speculative thinking. And so I sat and drank and tried to follow them.

1ST LANDOWNER:...our own generation too extreme when they define the ideal complexion for a woman. No one wants his wife or daughter brown from the sun. But am I perverse if I prefer a pallor that's not quite flawless? I'll speak frankly. All my life I've dreamed of a certain arrangement of...I refuse to use that banal word 'freckles'. Their colour must be a delicate gold, and I want to come across them in what seems an appropriate site. They lie far apart, but I can see them as a constellation if I wish. Gold on sheer white.

2ND LANDOWNER:...bustards of course, and plains-wanderers, and painted quail and stubble quail, and the brown songlark with that odd call it makes. And I ask myself...

3RD LANDOWNER:...with our cairns of stones on every hillside and plaques beside the roads and inscriptions still preserved on tree-trunks. But we forget that most of these men shouldn't be called plainsmen. This obsession with explorers. Please don't misunderstand me; it's a worthy task we've undertaken. But that vision of the plains we're all looking for—let's remember that the first explorers may not have been expecting plains. And many of them went back to their seaports afterwards. Certainly they boasted of what they had discovered. But the man I want to study is the one who came inland to verify that the plains were just as he'd hoped for. That vision we're all looking for...

4TH LANDOWNER: (Removes his jacket and rolls a shirtsleeve above his elbow. Stares at the skin of his forearm.) I have to admit that after all these years I know so little about my own skin. We're all plainsmen, always claiming that everything in sight is a landmark of something beyond it. But do we know what our own bodies are leading us towards? If I made maps of all your skins. I mean, of course, projections like Mercator's. If I showed them all to you, would you recognise your own? I might even point out to you marks like tiny scattered towns or clumps of timber on plains you've never thought of, but what could you tell me about those places?

1ST LANDOWNER: I'm speaking of my ideal woman, remember—the only woman that any of us speak about.

2ND LANDOWNER: Of course they can fly, and

there are trees enough on the plains. But they nest on the ground. And the bustard doesn't even make a nest— just a scrape or a little hollow in the dry soil. I'm not interested in arguments about evolution or instincts or that nonsense. All science is purely descriptive. What concerns me is the why of it. Why do some birds hide on the ground while their enemies threaten them? It must be a sign of something. The next time you see a bustard's nest, ask yourself why. Lie down and try to hide on the plain and see what happens.

5TH LANDOWNER: Surely we've neglected the first settlers—the men who stayed on the land they explored?

3RD LANDOWNER: But even after years on the plains they might have remembered another sort of land or the land they'd hoped to find if only the plains hadn't seemed to go on forever.

4TH LANDOWNER: I'm trying to remember those lines from 'A Parasol at Noon'—a neglected master-piece; one of the greatest romantic poems to come out of the plains. That scene where the plainsman sees the girl from a distance with all the paddocks swimming in heat haze. And don't bother to raise the old objection: that the poetry of that era turned us into parodies of ourselves, fixed in the posture of men forever looking into the distance.

6TH LANDOWNER: That scene is the *only* scene as I recall the poem. Two hundred stanzas on a woman seen from a distance. But of course she's hardly mentioned. It's the strange twilight around her that matters—the other atmosphere under the parasol.

4TH LANDOWNER: And as he walks slowly towards her he sees this aura, this globe of luminous air, under the parasol, which was silk, of course, and a pale yellow or green, and translucent. He never quite distinguishes her features in the glow. And he asks impossible questions: which light is more real—the harsh sunlight outside or the mild light around the woman? isn't the sky itself a sort of parasol? why should we think nature is real and things of our own making less so? And of course he wants to know why men of his kind can only possess what they come upon in dim alcoves of libraries with windows facing south onto deep, leaf-shaded verandahs.

2ND LANDOWNER: How much protection does the land offer us? We're all bustards or quail in our own way, seeing the plains as no one else does.

6TH LANDOWNER: Light of false suns informing works of art, / He always turned from. Yet a land apart, / Neither a plain of old nor yet a dream, / Had sometimes lured him with its secret gleam. / Now the frail silk directed to his eye / All the strange radiance of another sky.

5TH LANDOWNER: The fact is that the first settlers stayed here, presumably because the plains were the nearest approximation to the lands they'd been looking for. I can't believe that even our plains could equal that land we all dream of exploring. And yet I believe that land is only another plain. Or at least it must be approached by way of the plains around us.

3RD LANDOWNER: Who was it argued once that the plains ought to contain all the cities and mountains and seashores that we could hope to visit? In his novel he had every Australian living at the heart of some kind of plain.

6TH LANDOWNER: The parasol is the screen that each of us wants to keep between the real world and the object of his love.

2ND LANDOWNER: We talk of the way of the plains, but each of us thinks of his wife and daughters as waiting for him at the heart of a mansion of a hundred dim rooms. Most of our grandfathers were conceived in nests like quails' or bustards'.

4TH LANDOWNER: We've spent most of our lives out in the wind. We've seen the shadows of whole clouds lost on the miles of our grass. But we each remember, don't we, some afternoon on a verandah where the sunlight hardly reached through the leaves of creepers—or in a drawing room where the curtains stayed closed from early spring to late autumn. There were months when the plains seemed far away and we sat indoors every afternoon content to watch a certain pale face.

1ST LANDOWNER: The poets say we all worship

fair skin. But surely there are other reasons why we don't allow our wives and daughters to dress in bathing costumes? We know that the sunlight in summer can blind a person to the possibilities that lie behind the plains. And when we happen to see the turbulent air swirling like water above our land at noon, don't we turn away because it recalls the meaningless turmoil of oceans? In the hottest days of February we pity the poor coast-dwellers staring all day from their cheerless beaches at the worst of all deserts. We mock the poses they strike beside their oceans and profess not to understand their awe at a mere absence of land. Yet every man on the plains knows about those houses where the highest-priced women sit all day under lamps until every inch of their bodies is brown. Is there anyone here who hasn't once visited them and pretended for an hour that the plains mean nothing to him?

5TH LANDOWNER: You know the story of the man who was born too late to be the conventional sort of explorer. But he insisted that exploration was the only activity worthy of a plainsman. He marked out a square of his property and spent years drawing the most detailed maps of it. He named hundreds of features that you or I would have walked over without noticing. And he made notes and sketches of plants and birds as though no one before him had seen them. Then in his last years he locked away all his notes and maps and invited anyone who cared to explore the same place after him and write a description of it. When the two descriptions were compared, the differences between them would reveal the distinctive qualities of each man: the only qualities that he could claim as his own.

3RD LANDOWNER: I happen to believe myself that we're all explorers in our way. But exploration is much more than naming and describing. An explorer's task is to postulate the existence of a land beyond the known land. Whether or not he finds that land and brings back news of it is unimportant. He may choose to lose himself in it forever and add one more to the sum of unexplored lands.

4TH LANDOWNER: But the patrons of those places are mostly young men. Everyone here today can remember those other dreams that came to us in our hottest summers. Every plainsman has turned his back for a moment on the fernery or the summer-house, the white frocks and parasols, and stared after the north winds. The coast was always five hundred miles away, and most of us knew we might never see it. But that itch in our skin when we looked south—we told ourselves it could only be eased by salt breezes or tidal waters. And some of us even argued that the pallor of the women we had been promised in marriage would be even more desirable after we had enjoyed those brown bellies and thighs with coarse grit clinging to their film of transparent oil.

2ND LANDOWNER: And all this talk of being true to the plains. We refused years ago to enrol our daughters in the great schools near the coast because they might be sent out half-naked in the sun to play hockey. And yet we've all seen the mating dance of the bustard. I've watched it for hours, lying on my belly in the tussocks. No other bird works itself into such a state. If we were consistent in our arguments about being true to the plains, wouldn't we come out of our shadowy houses and couple on the grass with only the great distances to hide us?

5TH LANDOWNER: And yet the plains themselves haven't been thoroughly explored. Two years ago I retained a surveyor and an historian to prepare a map of all the strips of territory between the settled districts, all the pockets of scrub and timber on Crown lands, all the unfenced river frontages. We all see these places at the far ends of our properties, but we think of them as no more than the background to our characteristic landscapes. When the map is finished I hope to plot the route of a journey of a thousand miles. And when I make that journey I want to see, just once in the distance, some hint of a land that could be mine.

6TH LANDOWNER: But in the most notorious houses there were always some girls who kept their last inches utterly white. And you took care never to learn beforehand which girls they were. So that sometimes— while you indulged the most absurd of your childish fantasies and lost yourself in some mad ritual of the coast—just when you were about to possess whatever it was that had brought you so far from your own country, you might see the very colour you had betrayed.

3RD LANDOWNER: Send out your surveyors and plan your lonely journeys. You'll spend your life looking for the wrong kind of plains. Every morning after breakfast I spend just ten minutes walking around my collection from the great age of landscapes. When I step back from any one painting I close my eyes until I'm standing in front of the next. After all these years I know exactly how many paces will take me from one to another. I'm trying to piece together a plain where nothing exists but what artists claim to have seen. And when I've fitted those landscapes together into one great painted plain, then I'll step outside one morning and begin to look for a new country. I'll go in search of the places that lay just beyond the painted horizons; the places that the artists knew they were only able to hint at.

6TH LANDOWNER: Our fashionable poets tell us only of women swathed in silk against the sun. I read them too. I know that a distant figure, all in white, in the shadow of an immense house at the height of an afternoon, can give meaning to a hundred miles of grass. But I want to read those unpublished poems that surely have been written in rooms facing southwards. I want to read those poets who knew that their desires could lead them out of even the widest land. I'm not talking of those few fools who appear every decade or so urging us to set our passions free and to speak frankly before our women. There must have been many a man who knew, without leaving his own narrow district of the plains, that his heart enclosed every land he could have travelled to; that his fantasies of scorching sand and vacant blue water and bare brown skin belonged not to any coast but to some mere region of his own boundless plain. What did such poets discover in those palatial houses each night, walking ankle-deep in those gold carpets the colour of unlikely sand beneath mirrors prolonging the unsubtle hue of framed seascapes? I nodded to poets every week in long passageways of the house where I thought I was exploring some coast. But none of them has ever published his story. And yet only poetry could describe what we were really doing in those sweltering towns under skies filled with throbbing stars. All of those girls had been born on the plains. Most of them knew less than we did of the ways of the coast. But they struck those awkward poses that we demanded. When they lolled on the yellow carpet in their two-piece floral bathing costumes, and our fingers traced long, devious journeys across their burnt skin, we supposed we were escaping from the plains. And at the end, moaning to ourselves, we thought we had come into possession of something that only the coast-dwellers enjoyed. But a poet would have recognised that no man of the coast had ever been so privileged as to see his petty pleasures from the vantage point of the plains. And there were nights, as I said, when we found between our fingers the same pallor that was always kept hidden from us on the plains. Then we suspected that we were being mocked—that even in that game of the coast, on pretended sand beside painted waves, our women kept something of the plains about them.

2ND LANDOWNER: Who knows what a quail or bustard sees when it stands watching from the heart of its territory? Or when it struts for hours trying to impress its mate? Scientists have done experiments that make me wonder. They cut the head from a female and stuck it on a pole and the male went on dancing round it all afternoon, waiting for it to show some sign.

5TH LANDOWNER: Every plainsman knows he has to find his place. The man who stays in his native district wishes he had arrived there after a long journey. And the man who travels begins to fear that he may not find a fitting end to his journey. I've spent my life trying to see my own place as the end of a journey I never made.

7TH LANDOWNER: (Swings his legs over the side of the stretcher; strides to the bar and pours himself a whisky; begins talking as though he has missed none of the conversation so far.) A man can know his place and yet never try to reach it. But what does our petitioner think?

The man turned towards me but avoided my eyes. The others stopped talking and refilled their glasses.

From somewhere beyond the half-open door a shaft of rich light entered the room. A few mirrors, fortuitously placed, and perhaps a small, neglected window whose blind had been left undrawn, might have marked the route of the afternoon sunlight through the dim halls. The amber ray rested on the floor between the men, and some of them shifted their stools to make room for it. Then I stepped towards the centre of the bar to speak and the light was gone from among them. But for as long as I stood and talked, I felt myself distinguished by the sign of afternoon on my back.

I spoke quietly and looked most often at the seventh man, who was half a head taller than the others and the most attentive—although he frequently pressed his hand over his eyes in the pose he had held on the stretcher. I told them simply that I was preparing the script of a film whose last scenes would be set on the plains. Those same scenes were still not written, and any man present might offer his own property as a location. His paddocks with all their long vistas, his lawns and avenues and fishponds—all these could be the setting for the last act of an original drama. And if the man happened to have a daughter with certain qualifications, then I would be pleased to consult her and even to collaborate with her in preparing my last pages. I made this offer, I said, because the end of my story depended on a female character who must appear an authentic young woman of the plains.

All of them were listening. I knew from a faint quickening of interest that most of them were the fathers of daughters. I could even identify the men whose daughters complained often that all the vistas they saw in films seemed to end in far, wide places but never in plains like their own. It was these men I was trying to win over when I boasted that my film would show even the textures of grassblades in obscure hollows and of mossy rockfaces on bleak outcrops on a plain that any of them might recognise although none had seen more than fragments of it.

Looking at the first of the six men, I remembered their talk from the hour just past. I told them that all their particular concerns—the themes they discovered in the history of the plains or in the stuff of their own lives—would appear in my film as an arrangement of simple but eloquent images. For I too knew that whenever I approached a woman I wanted nothing better than to learn the secret of a particular plain. I too had studied the ways of birds and wanted to occupy a territory with boundaries and landmarks invisible to all but my own scattered kind. And I believed that every man was called to be an explorer. My own film would be in one sense the record of a journey of exploration.

Then I turned to the seventh of the great land-owners and declared that of all forms of art, only film could show the remote horizons of dreams as a habitable country and, at the same time, could turn familiar landscapes into a vague scenery fit only for dreams. I would go even further, I said, and claim that film was the one art form that could satisfy the contra-dictory impulses of the plainsman. The hero of my own film saw, at the furthest limits of his awareness, unex-plored plains. And when he looked for what he was surest of in himself, there was little more definite than plains. The film was the story of this man's search for the one land that might have lain beyond or within all that he had ever seen. I might call it—without pretentiousness, I hoped—the Eternal Plain.

The seventh landowner slammed his glass on the counter and turned away from me. He strode back to the stretcher and eased himself down on it. I said nothing more. I wondered whether I had offended the one man I wanted most to impress. And then he began to speak.

One hand was pressed again to his forehead and his voice was faint. I expected the six others to move towards the stretcher to hear him, but they seemed to have taken the man's lying down as a signal that their long session was over. Even the few who bothered to empty their glasses were gone from the room while I was wondering what I ought to say to them.

The man on the stretcher had kept his eyes covered. I coughed to let him know that I was still in the room, and leaned over him to catch his words. I recognised that I was meant to hear him, although he did not once acknowledge me. And for all his mumbling and pausing, I could not mistake his meaning.

He found much of what I had said outrageous. I knew, surely, that no film had ever been made with the plains as its setting. My proposal suggested that I had overlooked the most obvious qualities of the plains. How did I expect to find so easily what so many others had never found—a visible equivalent of the plains, as though they were mere surfaces reflecting sunlight? There was also the question of his daughter. Did I think that by persuading her to stand against a vista of a few paddocks and to look towards a camera I would discover about her what I would never in fact learn if I followed her for years with my own eyes? He believed, nevertheless, that I might one day be capable of seeing what was worth seeing. If he could forget my young man's eagerness to look at simple coloured images of the plains, he might concede that at least I was trying to discover my own kind of landscape. (And what mattered more than the search for landscapes? What distinguished a man after all but the landscape where he finally found himself?) Perhaps, young and blind as I was, I ought to present myself at his country seat at sundown on the following day. I would be treated as a guest for as long as I cared to stay. But I would do better to accept, in my own good time, a post in the household. My designation of this post would be for me to choose. He suggested 'Director of Film Projects' but expected that I would one day blush at it. My salary would be any reasonable amount over and above the expenses incurred in performing my duties. There would be, of course, no formal list of duties to restrict the scope of my work.

He dismissed me with a slight gesture. I left him still lying with his eyes covered and recalled, in the passage outside where the afternoon was tending towards evening, that he had not once met my own eyes.

*

I slept from early evening until just before sunrise. I walked from my bed out onto the balcony and watched for the dawn over the plains. I was surprised to find that the last minutes before dawn, even in that country, still set me hoping for something other than the usual sun to appear. And on that of all mornings it seemed odd to be seeing myself as a character in a film and the streets and gardens below me, already portentous enough, as scenery of redoubled significance.

Before packing the books and papers on my desk, I marked on a folder the label: LAST THOUGHTS BEFORE BEGINNING THE SCRIPT PROPER. Then, on a clean sheet inside the folder, I wrote:

In all the weeks since I arrived here I have looked out only twice from my balcony. It would have been a simple matter to explore those plains that begin at the end of almost every street of the town. But could I have possessed them as I always wanted to possess a tract of plains?

Tonight I will stand within sight of her plains at last. The first scenes of *The Interior* begin to unfold at last. Now I have only to set my notes in order and write.

Yet an old doubt returns. Is there anywhere a plain

that might be represented by a simple image? What words or what camera could reveal the plains within plains that I heard of so often these last weeks?

The view from my balcony—now, like some native plainsman myself, I see not solid land but a wavering haze that conceals a certain mansion in whose dim library a young woman stares at a picture of another young woman who sits over a book that sets her wondering about some plain now lost from sight.

In moods like this I suspect that every man may be travelling towards the heart of some remote private plain. Can I describe to others even the few hundred miles that I crossed to reach this town? And yet, why attempt to show them as soil and grass when someone far away might see them even now as only a sign of whatever I am about to discover?

And by now her father will have told her that I am journeying towards her.

*

In some of the better shops of the town I ordered a filing cabinet and stationery, a simple camera and ample colour film. I gave my address as the estate of my new patron and relished the respect it earned me. I let it be understood that some employee of the landowner would collect and pay for my goods in due course. I spoke as though I myself would not be seen in the town for many months at least.

It seemed the hottest day yet on the plains. Even before noon my friends had come in from the streets to their places at the bar where I had first met them. I learned from them that my destination was eighty miles from the town and beyond the barest of districts. And the afternoon sun would be in my face all the way. But I thought of my journey as a venture into obscure regions by a route that few knew of.

My companions on that last morning in the bar talked, as they so often did, of their own projects. A composer explained that all his tone-poems and symphonic sketches had been conceived and written within a few miles of his birthplace in one of the least populous quarters of the plains. He was trying to find the musical equivalent of the characteristic sound of his district. Strangers commented on the utter silence of the place, but the composer spoke of a subtle blend of sounds that most people habitually failed to hear.

When his music was performed, the members of the orchestra were stationed far apart among the audience. Each instrument produced a volume of sound that could be heard only by the few listeners nearest it. The audience was free to move around—as quietly or as noisily as they wished. Some were able to hear snatches of melody as subtle as the scraping together of grass-blades or the throbbing of the brittle tissue of insects. A few even found some spot from which more than one instrument was audible. Most heard no music at all.

Critics objected that no one from the audience or the orchestra could hope to hear whatever harmony might have resulted from themes that were barely stated. The composer had always maintained in public that this was just as he intended: that the purpose of his art was to draw attention to the impossibility of comprehending even such an obvious property of a plain as the sound that came from it.

But in private, and especially in the hotel where I spent the last hours before my journey, the composer regretted that he would never know what his works amounted to. During each rehearsal he wandered all over the almost empty hall hoping—quite unreasonably, he knew—to hear from somewhere a hint of the whole whose separate parts he knew so well. But he was seldom aware of any more than the trembling of a single reed or string. And he almost envied those who heard the play of the wind across miles of grass as no more than a tantalising silence.

I thought it fitting that my last hours in the town should be spent with an artist whose work was lost on the world. I had sometimes thought of *The Interior* as a few scenes from a much longer film that could only be seen from a vantage point that I knew nothing of.

Then, in the last half-hour before I left the hotel, a painter I had never seen before told me a story that no film-maker could ignore.

Years earlier this man had set out to paint what he called, for convenience, the landscapes of dreams. He claimed to have access to a country derived from his unique perceptions. It was superior to any country that others called real. (The only merit of so-called real lands, he said, was that people of dulled sensibility could find their way about in them by agreeing to perceive no more than did others of their kind.) He had doubted whether any but an alert few could make out the features of his land. Nevertheless, he undertook to represent it by the traditional means of paint on canvas, lessening its strangeness a little for the sake of those who saw only what they saw.

The painter's early works were well praised but, so he thought, misunderstood. Viewers and critics saw his layers of gold and white as a reduction of the plains to their essential elements and his swirls of grey and pale green as hints of what the plains might yet become. For him, of course, they were unmistakable landmarks of his private country. And to emphasise that the subject of his art was in fact an accessible landscape, he put into his later work a few obvious symbols—close approximations of forms common to both the plains and his own land.

These works of his 'transitional period', as it came to be called, earned still higher praise. Seizing on the trace of a pattern far out in a waste of orange and gamboge, the commentators spoke of his coming to terms with the traditions of the plains. And the freakish greenness that emerged from an excess of blue was taken to mean that he had begun to acknowledge the aspirations of his fellow plainsmen.

The painter saw that I was anxious to be away. He interrupted his story and predicted that I would find no new country wherever I travelled. When he heard of my film, he said that no film could show more than those sights that a man's eyes rested on when he had given up the effort to observe. I objected that the last sequence of *The Interior* would bring to light the strangest and most enduring of my dreams. The painter said that a man could dream of nothing stranger than the simplest image that occurred to another dreamer. And he went on with his story.

There had been further stages in what the critics called his development. But all that I need know was that he was now painting what were agreed to be inspired landscapes. For three years he had seldom left his studio, whose only window was overhung with dense evergreen leaves. When he had to walk through the town he kept his eyes away from the segments of plain that loomed at the end of almost every street. He asserted that now he saw nothing but the land he had once dreamed of. But each day he turned his eyes away from its familiar colours and shapes and composed on his canvas some view of a country that might only be dreamed of in the sort of land he now inhabited continually.

He showed me a small coloured reproduction of one of his best-known works. It seemed to me a crude imitation of one of the gilt-framed, glass-covered land-scapes I had seen in the furniture department of the town's largest store. While I tried to think of a comment, the artist looked hard at me and said that this was for many plainsmen the only place remote enough to be a setting for dreams.

When I was fifty miles away on the road to the location of my film, I wished I had asked the artist whether he knew that his purple hills and silvery stream could have passed for a view of Outer Australia.

*

I met her at dinner on my first evening in the great house. As the only daughter, she was seated opposite me, but we said little to each other. She seemed not much younger than I, and therefore not as young as I had wanted her to be. And her face was not quite so untroubled as I had hoped, so that I had to visualise anew some of the compelling close-ups in the final scenes of my film.

I arranged to take only my evening meal with the family and to spend most of my day in the library or my suite of rooms adjoining it on the upper floor of the north wing. But the family understood that I might be met with at odd times anywhere in the grounds or out on the estate. As an artist I was entitled to look for inspiration in unlikely places.

My patron, the girl's father, required me to drink with him for an hour or two on the verandah after dinner every evening. On the first night, the two of us sat just outside the french windows of the drawing room. The man's wife and daughter were still in the room with a few female guests. I knew there would be many evenings when the verandah was crowded with male guests and with clients of the same standing as myself. But on that first night, whenever the daughter looked out towards the moonlit plains she saw the dark figure of myself huddled in close conversation with her father.

Crickets chirped intermittently from the obscure lawns. Once, a plover raised its faint, frantic cry in some far paddock. But the immense silence of the plains was scarcely disturbed. I tried to visualise the bright window and the figures against it as they would have appeared from somewhere in the vast darkness before me.

*

Alone in my study towards midnight I began a new section of my notes in a folder labelled: REFLECTIONS FROM THE ULTIMATE (?) PLAIN. I wrote: The road to the estate was an offshoot from a deserted side-road whose signposts were sometimes vague and contradictory. And when I stopped at the front gate (I made sure of this) there was no house or shed or haystack to be seen in all the miles of land around. The place where I stood was at the bottom of a gentle hollow measuring perhaps a few miles from rim to rim. And within the circle of those horizons I was the only human soul. My patron's home, of course, was somewhere on the other side of the gate but certainly not within view. The driveway that led to it did not even point the way. It went behind a plantation of cypresses on the shoulder of a slight hill and did not reappear. As I drove in from the road I told myself I was disappearing into some invisible private world whose entrance was at the loneliest point on the plains.

Now what remains for me to do? I am so close to the end of my quest that I can scarcely recall how it began. She has spent all her life on these plains. All her journeys have begun and ended within this enormous, quiet country. Even the lands she dreams of have their own kinds of plain far out in the heart of them. There are no fit words to describe what I hope to do. Descry her landscapes? Explore them? I could hardly tell in words how I have come to know these plains where I first came upon her. Hopeless to speak yet of those stranger places beyond them.

First I must have an intimate understanding of her own territory. I want to see her against the backdrop of the few square miles that are hers alone—the slopes and flats and timbered watercourses that seem unre-markable to others but yield a hundred meanings to her.

Then I want to bring to light the plain that only she remembers—that shimmering land under a sky that she has never quite lost sight of.

And I mean to see still other lands that cry out for their explorer—those plains that she recognises when she gazes out from her verandah and sees anything but a familiar land.

Last of all I want to venture into the plain that even she is not sure of—the places she dreams of in the landscape after her own heart.

*

During my first months in the great house I suited my methods of work to the leisurely rhythms of the plains. Each morning I strolled a mile or so from the house and lay on my back and felt the wind or stared at the clouds creeping past me. Then the time I had spent on the plains seemed unmarked by hours or days. It was a trance-like period or a long succession of almost identical frames that could have comprised some minute or so in a film.

In the afternoons I explored the library, sometimes adding to the notes for my filmscript but more often reading from the published histories of the plains and the bound diaries and letters and family papers that my patron had made available. And there was an hour towards evening when I waited by a certain window to see the daughter of the house walking towards me across the acres of lawn from the stables after her daily ride towards some district I had yet to see.

Sometimes in those first months I was still reading among the shelves of material on the plains when I heard her calling to the half-tame quail and bustards on the far side of the ornamental lake. Then, when I hurried to the window and looked for her in the shady park, her figure was never quite distinct from the shadowy after-images of whatever I had been reading. Alone in the distance she might have been the woman of three generations before who had been addressed each day for fifteen years in a long letter that was never delivered. Or the images of shrubbery and sky in the lake beside her might have lain in one of the fanciful lands in the unpublished stories for children written by her great-uncle, reputedly the most pessimistic of the philosophers of the plains. Or creeping towards the hesitant, timid bustards, she might have been her imagined self—the girl I had read of in her earliest diaries, who went to live among the tribes of ground-dwelling birds to learn their secrets, so she said.

Towards the end of the summer my notes were so extensive that I sometimes put them aside and looked for simpler means of devising the opening scenes of my film. I would stand at the window, holding up against the glass a painting done by the young woman in the last years of her childhood, and trying to see some detail of the land outside as though it was suspended in the translucent swathes of faded paint. Sometimes I cut a piece from the paper so that a distant view of actual plains appeared at a significant point of a painting. Once, I pasted a detail from a painting onto the glass at the centre of a large rectangular blank in a different painting. When this arrangement was fixed to the window I walked slowly towards it, murmuring music appropriate to the first frames of a film concerned with memories and visions and dreams.

*

Late on an afternoon in autumn I got up from reading her pencilled notes in the margins of the collected essays of a forgotten traveller and natural philosopher. I strolled to the window as usual and saw her not far off. There were no obvious signs of autumn in that part of the plains. On the few exotic trees the leaves curled at their edges. Patches of lawn were littered with tiny unpalatable berries. And horizons seemed a little less vague.

I supposed it was the lack of something in the sunlight that made her face so surprisingly distinct as she walked towards the house. But I could not account for her looking up as she did, for the first time, at my window.

I was standing a few paces back from the glass but I made no move to step forward. In the shadows of some of the earliest works on the plains I struggled to memorise a sequence of images that occurred to me. At the beginning of a film, or at its end (or perhaps the same scene would serve for both), a young woman appeared out of some solitude among the plains. She approached a massive homestead. Rounding a certain wing of the building she glanced through the windows of a complex of rooms decorated with toys and a child's sketches in crayon and watercolour. She reached a thicket of shrubbery and gazed at a vista of garden, or of garden receding into the plains, that only she could see. (Her body came between the camera and whatever she looked at.)

Finally she went to the most exposed slope of the lawns. She moved indecisively, as though in search of something unmistakable (had she glimpsed it some-where before?) but nevertheless elusive.

A moment arrived when a watcher of the film might have decided that the young woman was not acting a part—that her uncertain movements were a genuine search for something that the author of the script had only been able to guess at.

And then the woman turned her face fully to the camera, and a watcher might have said she was not even one of those participants in a documentary film who try to behave freely with no thought of the cameras following them. She was looking at whoever observed her as though the thing she sought might lie in that direction. Or perhaps she was simply unsure of what was expected from her: of what the scriptwriter had in mind.

*

The daughter of my patron turned away at last from looking up at my window. When she was gone from sight, I carried a small table to the place near the window where I had stood while she looked up. I placed a chair on the table and draped my cardigan over the back of the chair. I stood beside the chair to be sure that it reached to the height of my shoulders.

I needed a head for my dummy. I taped a feather duster to the chair in the correct position. But I guessed that the dull tail-feathers of a bustard would be barely visible through the window, whereas my own face was noticeably pale. (It occurred to me that most of my days on the plains had been spent indoors.) The top drawer of my filing cabinet was half-full of unused paper for manuscripts and typing. I took a handful of crisp white sheets, moulded them loosely around the fronds of the duster, and then fixed them in place with tape.

I checked that the young woman had gone into her own wing of the building. Then I walked downstairs and along the paths to the spot where she had stood looking up. I stood there myself and stared at the library window.

I was surprised at the seeming darkness inside the library. I had always kept the blinds drawn in every window but that one. Yet at my desk I still felt in contact with the intense light of the plains. Now the window, enclosing only a sort of twilight, showed nothing of the room behind it—only an image of the sky above me.

I allowed myself to stand there for as long as she had stood. I saw that the far sheen of the reflected sky was not the uniform steely colour it had first seemed, but faintly streaked and mottled. I would have taken all the pale markings for remote shreds of cloud, except that as I walked away one of them remained fixed in the glass while the image of the sky around it changed with every step I took.

I had been watching the blurred whiteness that stood for my own face—the blank paper I had fastened to the dummy of myself. But the young woman who had come in from the plains that afternoon had seen my actual face, unless it had been obscured by the wisps of cloud in a reflected sky.

*

I returned to the library and dismantled the crude likeness of myself. The sheets of paper that had passed for my face were wrinkled and creased, but I carried them to the great central table where I had worked since midsummer. I sat down and tried to smooth the paper a little with my hands. And I stared for a long time at the pages, as though they were anything but blank. I even wrote on them—a few hesitant sentences—before I swept them to the floor and went on with my work.

{ *t w o* }

PRELIMINARY NOTE: After more than ten years on the plains I must still ask myself whether I can exclude from my life's work every appearance of the country whose most common name in this district is the Other Australia. My difficulty is not that the place is unknown or unfamiliar to the people around me. If that were so, I might practise a variety of deceits on a young woman who has lived all her life on the plains. I might present myself as a man distinguished by the strangeness of all he had seen in his time. (And

yet surely this would be impossible. Have I forgotten
one of the commonest qualities of plainsmen—their
stubborn refusal to allow that the unfamiliar has any
claim on their imagination simply because it is unfamiliar? How many afternoons have I spent in this very
library, unrolling the great maps of the regions of plains
so far discovered and admiring the work of the most
respected of the schools of mapmakers—those who
locate their improbable tribes and preposterous beasts
in the regions assumed to be best known, and who fill
the places left blank by other schools with features
meant to seem distressingly familiar?)

My difficulty is not that I must persuade an
audience of plainsfolk that a man such as myself might
once have entertained or studied in all seriousness or
even tried to sustain himself with the false notions, the
absurd distortions, that I once took for descriptions of
plains. Again, this library includes the usual obscure
alcove devoted to the works of those little-read scholars
who have seldom been adequately rewarded for their
pains—the men who forwent the satisfaction of

studying the genuine disciplines or the countless unsolved questions arising out of the plains and instead took as their province the illusory or spurious plains depicted and even esteemed by people who never had sight of anything approaching a plain.

I might consider it a difficulty that a few of the scenes from *The Interior* could be understood as a sequence of events in the life of a man who can still recall places far from the plains. But surely not even the least perceptive plainsman could take my patterns of images for an account of any kind of progress. I have to remind myself that I am far from the country whose people suppose that the story of a human heart can be no different from the story of the body that it informs. In this library I have come across whole rooms of works speculating freely on the nature of the plainsman. Many of the authors inhabit systems of thought that are bizarre, bewilderingly unfamiliar, perhaps even wilfully removed from common comprehension. But no writer I have yet found has tried to describe a plainsman as bound by the vicissitudes of his flesh—and certainly not those misfortunes that afflict each body in the years before the heart can properly sustain it.

Of course, the literature of the plains abounds in accounts of childhood. Whole volumes have expounded in profuse detail the topography of countries or continents as they were descried under faltering sunlight in the only hour when they were said to exist—some fortunate interval between almost identical days before they were engulfed by events too trivial even to be remembered. And one of the disciplines that most nearly resembles what is called philosophy in far parts of Australia is known to have originated in the comparative study of scenes recalled by one observer alone and accounts of those same scenes by the same observer after he had acquired the skill to attempt a fitting description of them.

The same discipline, in recent years, has shifted its emphasis. It was perhaps inevitable that commentators should feel a certain frustration with a subject whose data remained forever the property of a solitary observer. And the new branch of the subject undoubtedly produced a more satisfying body of speculation. It is not surprising that almost every cultivated plainsman reserves a shelf of his library for some of the many studies in this now-fashionable discipline. There is even a satisfaction in seeing so many of those volumes in a uniform edition with their striking black and lilac jackets. Where else but on the plains could a new publishing house establish in a few years a substantial prosperity and a widespread reputation by issuing almost exclusively long treatises investigating the choice of images used by the authors of those provoking essays known as remembrances of the misremembered?

I too have admired the tortuous arguments and detailed elaborations, the pointing-up of tenuous links and faint reverberations, and the final triumphant demonstrations that something of a motif has persisted through an immense body of digressive and even imprecise prose. And like the thousands of readers of those works, I have wondered at the speculations that lie at the heart of the subject they expound—the conclusions vehemently defended by men who admit them to be indefensible. Like most plainsmen I have no urge to adopt any of them. To claim that these delicately poised suppositions are somehow proven or compelling would seem to debase them. And anyone who did so would appear as some acquisitive hoarder of certainties or, worse still, as a fool trying to use words for the least appropriate of purposes—to justify an effect wrought by words.

One of the chief attractions of these remarkable conjectures is that no one is able to use them to alter his understanding of his own life. And it is this which adds immensely to the pleasure of plainsmen as they apply one after another of the newest theories to their own circumstances. What might not follow, they ask themselves, if there should be nothing more substantial in all our experience than those discoveries that seem too slight to signify anything apart from their own brief occurrence? How might a man reorder his conduct if he could be assured that the worth of a perception, a memory, a supposition, was enhanced rather than diminished by its being inexplicable to others? And what could a man not accomplish, freed from any obligation to search for so-called truths apart from those demonstrated by his search for a truth peculiar to him?

These are only a few of the implications of the science that seems, by a happy chance, the most practised and discussed on the plains at the very time when I am preparing a work of art to show what I and no other could have seen. I must remember, though, that more than a few landowners (and who knows how many among the shop assistants and primary school teachers and racehorse trainers whose reading and writing are done in private?) have already abandoned the new discipline. They are far from decrying it. On the contrary, they insist that they have been more thoroughly converted to it than those who argue its finer points in the correspondence columns of the weekly magazines and take pride in being photographed with the author of some lilac-and-black volume at a quail-shooting weekend or a woolshed ball. But these reluctant students believe that the subject, by its very nature, cannot be pursued so long as there are opportunities for people to compare their assessments of it or to reach even tentative agreement as to its claims.

These people are prepared to wait for some year or other in the far future. In that year, so they say, when the climate of ideas on the plains is half-way through one of its gradual but inevitable cycles, even though plainsmen might still prefer those prose-poems or sonatas or masques for marionettes or bas-reliefs that seem to emerge from the abyss between a man and his past, the great questions of the present day will seem distant and strange to anyone who still haunts the ruins of our present sciences.

None of the scholars I mention can even guess how many successive encroachments of afternoon sunlight on the shadowy corners of libraries will have bleached the glossy inks on the books that they open at last. These men talk instead of the peculiar pleasure of knowing, when they finally chance on some unforeseen correspondence between metaphors in the confessions of a forgotten writer, that their prized discovery is of no value to others. They may count as one of their choicest tokens of that private vision sought by all plainsmen something that was discarded or even discredited years earlier. And the most rewarding of all projects, they say, is to restore to its earlier lustre some relic from the history of ideas. No matter what uses you find for it, or what coruscations you bring to light in its long-obscured surface, you may always enjoy a pleasant mistrust of your estimation of it. The insights you would like to cherish for their completeness may one day be newly enlarged by the merest footnote found in some outdated text. And even though you delight in your possession of neglected notions and discarded ideas, you must acknowledge that someone before your time has considered them in a different light.

And I remind myself again—in all the arts and sciences that spring from the plainsman's awareness of loss and change no thinker has seriously entertained the possibility that the state of a man at some moment in his life may be illuminated by a study of the same man at some moment said, for convenience, to have preceded the moment in question. For all their pre-occupation with childhood and youth, plainsmen have never considered, except as illustrations of self-evident falsehoods, the theory that the flaws in a man result from some primal mishap, or its corollaries, that a man's life is a decline from a state of original satisfaction and that our joys and pleasures are only a compromise between our wants and our circumstances.

Not only my years of reading but my long conversations with plainsmen—even the head of this house, my unpredictable patron, who only visits the library nowadays to search for colour plates in histories of certain ceramic styles—assure me that people here conceive of a lifetime as one more sort of plain. They have no use for banal talk of journeys through the years or the like. (I am surprised almost daily to learn how few plainsmen have actually travelled. Even in their Golden Age, the Century of Exploration, for every pioneer who found a way to some new region there were scores of men who earned equal fame by describing their own narrow districts as though they lay still beyond the farthest of the newly discovered lands.) But in their speech and song they allude constantly to a Time that converges on them or recedes from them like some familiar but formidable plain.

When a man considers his youth, his language seems to refer more often to a place than to its absence, and to a place unobscured by any notion of Time as a veil or barrier. The place is inhabited by people privileged to search for its particularity (that quality which obsesses plainsmen as the idea of God or of infinity has obsessed other peoples) as readily as the man of the present might try to divine the special identity of his own place. Much is made, of course, of the failure of each—the man and the young man—to comprehend his unique situation. The two are often compared with dwellers in neighbouring regions who try to map all the plains they might find necessary or all they would be content to know, and who agree that each may include parts of the other's borders in his own map, but who find at last that their two charts cannot be brought together neatly—that each has argued for the existence of an ill-defined zone between the last places that he could wish for and the first of those that he has no claim to. (Luckily my present task excuses me from concerning myself with that sizable school of thinkers who insist that all learning—and even, some have said, all art— should be derived from those shadowy areas that no one properly occupies. I must one day satisfy my curiosity, though, about their theory of the Interstitial Plain: the subject of an eccentric branch of geography; a plain that by definition can never be visited but adjoins and offers access to every possible plain.)

So, when my patron broods over the uneven translucence and the manifold intensities of green and gold in the glaze of tiles that resemble only slightly a kind that he saw and handled years ago, he is not in any crude sense trying to 'recapture' some experience from the past. If he thought in that fashion he might stroll to some of the porticos and courtyards in the southeast wing where the very tints that he strives to visualise, reflecting the afternoon sunlight or the reflected remnants of that light, allow even me to admire a conjectural greenness that may never appear again among those scrupulously preserved pillars and pavements and pools. And his hours of silent study are no proof that he repudiates the appearances and sensations arising from any plain of the moment. If I know him, he thinks quite dispassionately of some other afternoon in courtyards where even the great silences of the plains are walled out for the sake of a more provoking silence still and where the perhaps inimitable lustre of glazed clays enhances a green and a gold more remote from common preferences than even the rarely seen hues of the empty grasslands on their farther side. He wants of all that is irretrievable only that it should seem to be bounded on all sides by familiar terrain. He wants the schematic arrangement of his own affairs to equal that pattern so favoured by plainsmen—a zone of mystery enclosed by the known and the all-too-accessible. And being the man he is, he almost certainly intends these quiet afternoons to demonstrate a further refinement of the famous pattern. The man calmly studying the tints and textures of his simply decorated tiles allows that the full meaning of what lies seemingly within reach of his hands or within range of his eyes rests with another man who runs his fingers over the surfaces of tiled walls warm from the afternoon sun and whose sensations include an awareness of still another man who comes near to interpreting a conjunction of fading sunlight and glowing colours but suspects that the truth of such a moment must lie with a man beyond him who sees and feels and wonders further.

I sometimes doubt whether my patron conceives of Time in the orthodox fashion of the school of opinion he claims to adhere to. In his occasional discussions with me he defends 'Time, the Opposite Plain' against the other four theories currently propounded. But I notice in some of his arguments an excess of neatness. I know enough of the habits of thought of plainsmen to expect them usually to prefer those theories that fall short of a complete explanation for the problem at hand. My patron's show of delight in the symmetry and completeness of what he perceives as Time may indicate that he is privately investigating one of the other popular theories or, more likely, that he has been compelled to become one of those doctrinal solitaries aware of a Time whose true configurations only they perceive. Until recently they were regarded as highly as the followers of the five schools. But since some of the more zealous have made their private labyrinths of Time the settings for their poetry and prose and for those newer works (some hopelessly fragmented, others almost unbearably repetitive) that still await acceptable names, critics—and even the usually tolerant reading public—have become impatient.

This may not be because ordinary plainsmen find such practices confusing or destructive of the scope and variety of their own favoured methods for elaborating on the theme of Time. Still, the subject seems one of the few in which plainsmen prefer not to trust to the insights of the solitary seer. Perhaps, as some commentators have asserted only recently, the five major theories are still so incomplete, so fraught with areas of vagueness, that even the most original thinker ought to locate his paradoxical landscapes and ambiguous cosmologies within their ample voids. Or perhaps those who most protest—although they include almost equal numbers of followers of the five schools—are secret believers in another theory that has never yet been clearly expressed. This is the self-defeating proposition that Time can have no agreed meaning for any two people; that nothing can be predicated of it; that all our statements about it are designed to fill up an awesome nullity in our plains and an absence from our memories of the one dimension that would allow us to travel beyond them. In that case, the opponents of the wayward investigators are only guarding against the likelihood that one of those heretics might find the means of suggesting this proposition to others. (It would almost certainly be achieved through poetry or some abstruse fictional narrative. Plainsmen are seldom won over by logic. They are too easily distracted by the neatness of its workings, which they use for devising ingenious parlour games.) And the fear of these opponents would be that the new view of Time might do away with those elaborate conceits employed by plainsmen in their countless investigations of the mutability of all things. They might find themselves all dwellers on plains of such permanence that only those men survived who could deceive themselves with hours of their own making or feign a belief in years that no one else guessed at.

Some years ago I was tempted to visit that corner of the library where the great works on Time spilled out from the ranks of shelves once thought ample to accommodate them in what was then the foreseeable future. I noticed that the same corner attracted the wife of my patron on her daily visits to the library. She was a woman no older than myself and still beautiful according to the conventions of the plains. She rarely examined a book from the towering stacks around her—only stared at an assortment of titles and handled an occasional coloured jacket. She paid much attention to the curtains along the western wall of the room. Sometimes she drew the massive honey-coloured hangings closer together so that the light surrounding her seemed suddenly richer but perhaps no less transitory. Or else she parted those same curtains, and the glare from the declining sun and the inevitable bare grasslands effaced the complex radiance from the hundreds of works devoted to Time.

I knew almost nothing about her. In all my private interviews with her husband (once a month in the suite of rooms that he calls his studio) he had never mentioned the wife who has spent so many afternoons in this house that she might have seen by now the refracted sunlight from three thousand separate plains through each of its countless windows.

I knew that my patron followed the custom, common to all eminent plainsmen, of paying an oblique tribute to a nameless wife in every work of the art that he privately practised. In my patron's case, however, the references may have been more than usually obscure. If he had spent his silent days at the verses of a ballad, I might have been a little nearer to knowing something of the woman's story. For each ballad of the plains returns and returns from its interminable paraphrasings and irrelevancies to a few unmistakable motifs. Or if he had frequented those neglected rooms where the immense looms stand as his grandfather left them, I might have seen how his wife should have appeared in a setting he envisaged for the two of them. For the weavers of the plains make only a pretence of hiding their female subjects among scenes they can never have witnessed. But the only man who might have interpreted this woman's reveries, as she stood between the uniform glow from the plains and the many-coloured sheen on the commentaries on Time, produced nothing more eloquent than murals of green glaze and figurines posed ambiguously. I knew from chance remarks of his late at night what an expanse of meaning he hoped to suggest with those reticent and cryptic works. And I knew that plainsmen commonly consider all art to be the scant visible evidence of immense processes in a landscape that even the artist scarcely perceives, so that they confront the most obdurate or the most ingenuous work utterly receptive and willing to be led into bewildering vistas of vistas. Yet I stood in quiet courtyards between far wings of this house, with no view of plains to distract me, and watched how each thickness of variable cloud at my back effected, in the greenish wall before me, now an illusion of boundless depths and now the absence of anything approaching an horizon. And I traced all the while whatever had the appearance of a theme in that uncertain region: following as far as its seeming source some flaw or fingermark that could have suggested this or that human propensity wavering but persisting in a landscape which itself came and went; discerning a play of powerful opposites in the alternate predominance of differing textures; or deciding that whatever seemed to point to some unique perception of a private terrain might suggest in another light that the artist had failed to see the scattered vestiges of what passed for another country with another observer.

And so I could do no more than speculate about the years when the man and his wife went on standing at their separate stations (she near the western windows of the library between a wall patterned intricately with colours of books she rarely opened and a plain that turned ponderously yet again away from the sun with its import still far from obvious, and he in a walled courtyard with his back all day to the few windows where cobwebs dangled before aspects of plains and his face close to the coloured clays where he claimed to see what only his years had disclosed) and each behaved as though there was yet time to hear from the other a form of words acknowledging some of those possibilities that had never been realised for as long as each had despaired of arranging such things in a form of words.

There were days, though, when the woman walked even further off among the rooms given over to Time and sat reading in one of the smaller bays facing south among the works of lesser philosophers. (Even at this distance from the Other Australia, I sometimes recall what was described as philosophy there. And almost daily, as I pace some unfamiliar path from my table here, I am pleasantly surprised to see, in the rooms and bays reserved for philosophy, works that would have been given any name but that in my native district.) The books she read most often would perhaps be called novels in another Australia, although I cannot believe they would find publishers or readers in such a place.

But on the plains they make up a well-respected branch of moral philosophy. The authors concern themselves with what they call, for convenience, the soul of the plainsman. They say nothing of the nature of any entity corresponding to this term, leaving the matter to the acknowledged experts—the commentators on the most arcane of poetry. But they describe minutely some of its undoubted effects. These scholars isolate from their own experience (and from each other's—for they remain a closely knit, almost exclusive, group, marrying the sisters and daughters of colleagues and rivals, and inducting their own children into their demanding profession) certain states of regretfulness, unfulfilment or deprivation. They then examine these states for evidence of some earlier state which seemed to promise what was never subsequently realised. In almost every case the vindicators of the evanescent, as they are sometimes called, establish that the earlier experience did not in fact portend any increase in satisfaction or any state of contentment in an unspecified future. The writers do not go on to argue that the later experiences are of no value or that a plainsman ought to avoid all expectation of future consolation, and certainly not that no lasting pleasures are available. Instead they draw attention to a recurrent pattern in human affairs—the fleeting perception of a promise of boundless good followed by the arrival of that good in the affairs of someone who neither foresaw it nor recognises it as a good. They claim that the proper response to this is to yield to the intensity of all seeming disappointments, not with a sense of having been deprived of some rightful happiness but because the continued absence of a conjectured enjoyment defines it more clearly.

I surmised, then, that the woman who sat each afternoon wondering what had become of a husband and wife she had once caught sight of on a singular plain persuaded herself that she had erred in supposing she might one day approach them or their peculiar land-scape. Whenever she made her way, through empty corridors and past silent rooms where she had once expected to utter or to hear the phrases that would link the plains all around her with a plain she had only divined, to the windowless corner and the astringent consolation of the so-called philosophers of the lost, I assumed that she had already been won over by their doctrines. In that case, she dwelt, while I watched her furtively, not on the uncertain distance between her present circumstances and whatever mansion and far-flung estates a certain other woman had come to occupy, but on ample unspecified plains she might still not have entered. For the thinkers of that school disregard the question whether a possibility, once entertained, may seem one day to correspond to some meagre arrangement of events. They give all their attention to the possibility itself and esteem it according to its amplitude and to the length of time for which it survives just beyond reach of the haphazard disposition of sights and sounds which is called, in careless speech, actuality, and has been considered, perhaps even by a few plainsmen, to represent the extinction of all possibilities.

The woman might therefore have considered the chief advantage of so many years spent among unlooked-for plains, with a man who had still not explained himself, to be that it had once allowed her to postulate the existence of a woman whose future included even the unlikely prospect of half a lifetime spent among unlooked-for plains with a man who would never explain himself.

But the philosophy of the plains includes so much of what I once thought the subject-matter of fiction that my patron's wife might have read long before certain treatises that I had glanced at in the years when I allowed myself to follow ramified ways leading from footnote to footnote in bulky but marginal studies of Time, the Plain Beyond Reach. (These are diffuse accounts of events that could have occupied only moments in the lives of those concerned but are described as the chief happenings in their histories.) She would surely have read, I thought, at least one of those accounts of a man and a woman who met only once and accepted that so much was promised to them by the decorous looks and words they exchanged that they should not meet again. And, as she followed the accounts of the later lives of those couples, she must have understood how her own years in this house were little part of her own story. The afternoons of unbroken silence, the briefly lambent twilights, and even the mornings that seemed about to restore to the plains something that she had not quite despaired of—these were the merest hints of a life that might have been: of the countless landscapes brought into being years before by a wordless exchange between herself and a young man who might have led her anywhere but to these plains where he had promised to lead her. Such a sympathy seemed to grow between us (although we never spoke, and even when one of us looked across the library the other's eyes were always turned to some page of a text or some page awaiting its text) that I hoped she might even believe her years in this district had a worth such as her favourite authors awarded to all lives that seemed to arrive at nothing. For some of those writers she seemed to prefer look on much of what is called history as a hollow show of gestures and ill-considered utterances maintained partly to fulfil the petty expectations of those preoccupied with what can be safely predicted, but chiefly to provide scope for the perceptive to foresee what they know can never come about. A few of those same philosophers would even argue that the woman's years of disquiet were, of all conceivable eventualities, the only sequel appropriate to the moment when a young woman saw as he might never appear again a man who saw her as she might never appear again. For them (their works are obscurely placed on a remote shelf, but it was at least possible that she had come across them once in all the years she had spent in this library) a lifetime is no more and no less than an opportunity for proving such a moment utterly unconnected with all those that follow it and is the more to be valued for every uneventful year which emphasises that proof.

We met, of course, and exchanged polite words in other rooms at other hours. But seeing her in distant corners of the library I felt myself barred from approaching. For a long time I was constrained by the slightness of my own ideas as they would have seemed if I had uttered them in those surroundings. I believed

I had no right to speak unless it was to address myself to some proposition contained in one of the volumes around me. The silence that persisted in those rooms I heard as the pause that a speaker allows when his argument has unrolled to its end and he waits defiantly for the first of his questioners, except that the tension in this case was compounded by the hugeness of the throng of speakers and by the scores of years in which the silence had still not been broken.

But as months passed and she came almost every afternoon to sit between me and the shelves labelled TIME, I was more and more compelled to declare something to her. I sensed between us the mass of all the words we might have spoken as a stack of unopened volumes as daunting as any of the actual shelves that stood above each of us. It was probably this that suggested to me the scheme I decided on. As soon as I had finished my preliminary notes for *The Interior*, and before I began work on the filmscript itself, I would write a short work—probably a collection of essays— which would settle things between the woman and myself. I would have it published privately under one of the seldom-used imprints that my patron reserves for his clients' work in progress or marginalia. And I would so arrange the ostensible subject-matter of the work that the librarians here would insert a copy among the shelves where she spends her afternoons.

I foresaw this much of my scheme happening as I had planned it. The only uncertain item was the last— I had no way of ensuring that the woman would open my book during her lifetime. I might have observed her every afternoon during the five or ten years that I planned to spend in this house and never have seen her come remotely near the words that could have explained my silence.

But I was not bothered for long by the likelihood of her never reading my words. If everything that passed between us existed only as a set of possibilities, my aim should have been to broaden the scope of her speculations about me. She ought to acquire not specific information but facts barely sufficient to distinguish me. In short, she should not read a word of mine, although she should know that I had written something she might have read.

I intended for a short time, therefore, to write the book and to have it published but to release only a handful of copies to reviewers (and only after receiving a written undertaking from each that the book should not be circulated) and one copy to this library. On the day when that copy was first shelved I would remove it quietly into my own safekeeping after making certain that it had been fully described in the catalogue.

Not even this scheme satisfied me for long. So long as a single copy of my book remained extant, our sympathy for one another was circumscribed. Worse still (since I wanted our relationship to be unrestricted by common notions of time and place), no one after our deaths could be sure that she had not found and opened the book during her lifetime. I thought of issuing only one copy—to the librarians here—and of then removing and destroying it as soon as the catalogue entry was completed. But someone in the future could still surmise that a copy existed (or had once existed) and that the woman it was meant for had at least glanced at it.

I amended my scheme once again. Somewhere in the catalogue here is a list of notable books never acquired by this library but held in other private collections in great houses of the plains. I would keep to myself every copy of my book and insert in that list an entry stating that a copy was housed in a fictitious library in a non-existent district.

By this time I had begun to ask myself why the woman herself might not have devised a book to explain her position to me. It was my own reluctance to search for this book that finally persuaded me to do what I did, which was to write no book and to put abroad no suggestion that I had ever written a book or intended to write a book.

Having reached this decision I hoped that both the woman and I would be able to leave one another undisturbed in our separate zones of the library, sure of the possibility that we might have met as young man and woman and married and learned of each other what two such people would have learned in half a lifetime. But I soon discovered a source of discontent in this (as, perhaps, in all possibilities). When I entertained even the vaguest thoughts of the two of us as man and wife I had to allow that even such people could not have existed without a possible world to counterbalance what was for them the actual. And in that possible world were a couple who sat silently in separate bays of a library. We knew almost nothing of one another and we could not conceive of things happening otherwise without violating the poise of the worlds that surrounded us. To think of ourselves in any other circumstances would betray the people who might have been ourselves.

I arrived at this understanding some time ago. Since then I have tried to avoid those rooms that grow steadily more crowded with works to explain away Time. Sometimes, however, on my way past that region of the library, some rearrangement of the newest stacks leads me through circuitous ways past a room where I formerly watched the woman. She sits further off than I seem to remember her, and already the changed scheme of shelves and partitions has separated her from me by the first of what will become, inevitably, a maze of pathways among walls of books as this wing of the library becomes the visible embodiment of one or another of those patterns attributed to Time in the volumes standing quietly at the heart of it.

I may take pleasure occasionally in the sight of her so close to the crowded shelves that the pallor of her face is momentarily tinted by a faint multiple glow from the more hectic of the jacketed volumes around her. But I prefer myself not to be seen in the places given over to Time, no matter how nearly I might seem to approach the plainsman's view of all that might have happened to me. I have a fear, perhaps unreasonable, of finding myself beguiled by images of what almost came to pass. Unlike a true plainsman, I do not care to inspect too closely those other lives lived by men who might almost have been myself. (It was surely this fear that first brought me to the plains: to the one place where I need not concern myself with such possibilities.) The countless volumes of this library are close-set with so much speculative prose; so many chapters after chapters appear in parentheses; such glosses and footnotes surround the trickles of actual text that I fear to discover in some unexceptional essay by a plainsman of no great reputation a tentative paragraph describing a man not unlike myself speculating endlessly about the plains but never setting foot on them.

So I keep away nowadays from the volumes in which Time itself is made to appear as one more sort of plain. I have no wish to be seen, even by that silent woman among those lengthening vistas of provocative titles, as a man in sight of Time, the Invisible Plain, or approaching Time, the Plain Beyond Reach, or finding his way back from Time, the Pathless Plain, or even surrounded by Time, the Boundless Plain. When I explain myself at last to plainsfolk I must appear as a man secure in his own view of Time. The light around me will be dim. Perhaps the place will be some chamber from among the many I have yet to visit in this very library. For all my audience knows of the plains outside, long afternoons may have come and gone. All that concerns them are images from the film that tells of a man seeing the plains from an unheard-of vantage point. And even if they glance from those images to the man who composed them, they will see only my face faintly lit by the wavering colours of scenes from a Time vaguely familiar to all of them.

Now, no longer obliged to explain myself to my patron's wife, I have to overcome the doubts that sometimes occur to me at the monthly dusks, as they are called. I do not believe that anyone at those brief, amicable gatherings intends to unsettle me. We sit, so often in silence, in the main drawing room—the only such room with no view of the plains but instead a prospect of tall hedges and dense, clipped trees meant to encourage freer, more speculative thought by its suggestion that the unimaginable has happened after all and we are separated from our plains by uncongenial forests of uncertain extent or by the distractions of contrived landscapes. And as soon as my patron has determined that the room is quite in darkness (having failed to identify the small framed landscape placed by a servant, according to custom, in the hands of the nearest guest) we leave—entirely without ceremony, but thinking, as the spirit of the occasion requires, of what we might have learned if someone had declared himself during that hour of fading twilight.

How could I be disturbed by the few words that are spoken at those dusks? Each man present is careful to say only what is most predictable—to make the briefest and most banal of comments—and to maintain the impression that he has accepted his formal invitation and travelled for perhaps half a day to say and to hear nothing of consequence. My doubts arise instead during the long silences when I compare myself, still intent on composing a work of art that will startle, with the more celebrated of the guests.

My patron invites to his dusks some of the famous recluses of the plains. What can I say of them, when their aim is to say and do nothing that can be described as an achievement? Even the term 'recluse' is hardly apt, since most of them will accept an invitation or receive a guest rather than attract notice by untoward aloofness. They affect no shabbiness in their dress and no uncouthness in their manners. Of those I have met, the only one known for eccentric behaviour is the man who travels every year at the beginning of spring with a servant on a weeks-long journey across the plains and back again, never parting the dark curtains around him in the rear compartment of his car and never leaving his hotel room in any town where he breaks his journey.

Since none of these men has ever spoken or written a word to explain his preferring to live unobserved and untroubled by ambition in some modestly furnished rear suite of his unremarkable house, I can only say that I sense about each of them a quiet dedication to proving that the plains are not what many plainsmen take them for. They are not, that is, a vast theatre that adds significance to the events enacted within it. Nor are they an immense field for explorers of every kind. They are simply a convenient source of metaphors for those who know that men invent their own meanings.

Sitting among those men at twilight, I understand

their silence to assert that the world is something other than a landscape. I wonder whether anything I have seen is a fit subject for art. And the truly perceptive seem to me those who turn their faces away from the plains. Yet the next morning's sunrise dispels these doubts, and at the moment when I can no longer look at the dazzling horizon I decide that the invisible is only what is too brightly lit.

No, (to return to the subject of this note) there is little chance of plainsmen mistaking what I have to show them for some sort of history. Even if I presented them with what I considered a narrative of exploration—a story of how I first surmised the existence of the plains, how I made my way here, how I learned the ways of the region where I announced myself as the maker of a film, and how I travelled further still to this region that once seemed impossibly remote—even then my audience, accustomed to seeing the true connections between apparently consecutive happenings, would see my true meaning.

No, absurd as it may seem, my chief difficulty—

and what may well be the subject of further notes before my work itself begins—is that the young woman whose image should have meant more than a thousand miles of plains might never understand what I want from her.

From just one of all the windows in all the rooms of this library, I sometimes see my patron's eldest daughter on some pathway amongst the nearest of the conservatories. (I must examine before long the matter of her preference for the humid avenues of those glazed pavilions rather than the windy clearings in the park among trees native to every district of the plains.) She is little more than a child, which is why I take care not to be seen observing her, even from such a distance. (There is one glasshouse in which she stands for long intervals. If I could find some window in some part of the library still unknown to me, I could stare down on her for as long as I chose. Even if she turned away from looking at some flower unsuited to the plains and glanced upwards, she would surely see nothing of me among whatever reflections of exotic foliage and her own pale face hung in the air beyond the tinted glass of her own enclosure and short of the panes before my own shadowy station.) Even so, I have tried to persuade her father to offer to her tutors some of my studies of aspects of the plains. I hope to make her curious about the man she sees only from a distance on the few formal occasions when an eldest child is admitted to the drawing rooms, and about the means he is reputed to have devised for rendering the most obscure of plains. But my patron has allowed me only once to submit to her principal tutor some of my findings and a brief description of the project I am still preparing.

In all the months since then, I have been shown in return only a short extract from a series of commentaries written by the girl on the work of a compiler of sketchbooks of regions of the plains. I could not miss the brief reference to myself (in her faultless handwriting) but it gave me no encouragement. If she had misunderstood only the more particular of my aims, I might have prepared for her a clearer exposition of them. But she seems blind even to the reason for my presence in her house. This is not the place to examine the fanciful image she entertains of me. I will note only that even the least of her expectations would barely be fulfilled if I disregarded the long story of my stay on the plains and presented myself simply as a curious traveller from outermost Australia.

{three}

I kept to the library, although it wasn't always the secure refuge I needed. Admittedly my patron rarely bothered me in the evenings. I might have set the clusters of lamps blazing in all the chambers and passageways of the place and wandered all night undisturbed among rooms of books I hadn't yet examined. But I preferred to work by daylight when the tall windows on one side, and the ranks of variegated volumes on the other, allowed me to think of myself as still poised between two enormities.

The two that then confronted me seemed more forbidding than in earlier years. Through many of the windows I saw, when the blinds and drapes were not drawn, what I could only describe as hills—a range of slopes and folds with close-set tufts of treetops filling the deepest valleys between them. The people of the house had been puzzled by my interest in those hills. No one regarded them as any sort of landmark. Their whole expanse was named for the five creeks that rose among them, and when I had suggested that the landscape was unusual for the plains I was reminded that I was now in a district where people often lost sight of intervening features in their concern for the larger plains as they understood them. What I would have called a distinctive region inviting study was only a detail of the plains properly considered. And in the other direction, among the rooms of books, I found much to confuse me. I had thought I knew enough of the writing of the plains to follow in any library the subjects nearest to my own life's work. But in those mazes of rooms and annexes, the categories I had at last become familiar with were apparently disregarded. The owner of the huge collections and his resident librarians and keepers of manuscripts seemed to have agreed on a system of classification that intermingled works never linked by any conventions of the plains as I knew them. Sometimes of an afternoon, aware on the one hand of the disconcerting ridges between my windows and a reputed horizon and, on the other, of the continual blurring of distinctions among the unpredictable sequences of titles, I wondered whether all my investigations so far had been mere glances at the deceptive surfaces of plains.

Sometimes this doubt bothered me for so long that I began to hope my patron would invite me soon to another of his 'scenes', although these had seemed tiresome distractions in my early years on that estate.

There were weeks when I spoke to no one in the great house. I sat and read and tried to write and waited for a clear sign of what I could only call the invisible event that was bound to involve me. Then, on the last morning of a spell of fine weather, when the sky was edged with the haze of a storm that would be all day in coming, and I might have looked forward to an after-noon when my revelation would hang poised about me like the promise of change in the oppressive air, then the message would come that I was required at a scene.

The word had once seemed to me the least felici-tous of the many usages peculiar to the family and the retinue of my patron of those days. I took it at first to be no more than a capricious substitute for the several common terms describing the elaborate day-long expe-ditions of families to nameless sites in far corners of their lands. I had taken part in such outings with other great families and enjoyed especially their habit of retiring for most of the day inside their huge window-less tents, drinking quietly but relentlessly, hearing the sweep of grass against the outer sides of their translucent walls, and affecting not to know where among miles of such ruffled grasses they might have been. (For some of them it was no affectation. They had begun drinking at breakfast, while the cars and vans were being loaded and the women were far away behind closed doors dressing in the formal style that was always observed on those days. And there were others who perhaps guessed which of a thousand similar places they had settled in, but fell into a drunken sleep, still sitting upright and correctly dressed, on the long journey home and remembered nothing next day.)

But I had learned in time that my patron's talk of scenes was more than an earnest attempt to establish the word as part of the dialect of his region. The man spent much of the afternoon assembling men and women from the throng of guests in poses and attitudes of his own choosing and then taking photographs. His camera was a simple outdated model picked in haste from a half-dozen that he carried always in the cavernous luggage compartment of his car. The film was from a stock of black-and-white rolls bought in a distant town from some shopkeeper used to accommodating the unprofitable whims of the great landowners. The prints that resulted from these tedious tableaux were afterwards described without enthusiasm by the few people who troubled to inspect them.

The man who strode among the reluctant subjects of these photographs, pausing to gulp from the glass still in his hand or to consult the sheaf of scribbled notes poking from his jacket, had confided to me that he cared nothing for the so-called art of photography. He was prepared to argue, against those who made pretentious claims for the output from cameras, that the apparent similarities in structure between their ingenious toys and the human eye had led them into an absurd error. They supposed that their tinted papers showed something of what a man saw apart from himself—something they called the visible world. But they had never considered where that world must lie. They fondled their scraps of paper and admired the stains and blotches seemingly fixed there. But did they know that all the while the great tide of daylight was ebbing away from all they looked at and pouring through the holes in their faces into a profound darkness? If the visible world was anywhere, it was somewhere in that darkness—an island lapped by the boundless ocean of the invisible.

The man had told me this in a sober moment. But at his scenes, drinking himself steadily towards unconsciousness and snaring great cones of light from the plains in his shabby cameras, he seemed to mock himself. I had noticed from the first that scenes were never arranged on days of unfailing brightness. Always, when the numerous parties assembled on the leafy verandahs and broad driveways, the sky further inland was uncommonly hazy. The sunlight might persist until late afternoon, but the turbulent clouds filled more and more of the sky. The man who had chosen that day for his scene went on urging his family and guests to enjoy themselves in the still-languid air. But then he would take me aside as though only I could understand his secret purpose.

'The encroaching darkness,' he might say, gesturing towards the half of the sky that was already occupied by cloud. 'Even a place as huge and bright as the plains can be blotted out from any direction. I stare at this land now, and every glowing acre of it sinks into my same old private darkness. But others may be looking at the plains too. That weather—it's only a sign of all the invisible territory around us all at this very moment. Someone has been looking at us and our precious land. We're disappearing through the dark hole of an eye that we're not even aware of. But more than one can play at that game. I've still got my toy—my camera that renders things invisible.' And he might point the box awkwardly at me and ask did I fancy an expedition into the unseen world.

In the early evening, while the storm was overhead and the people around the replenished tables stared silently out from their tents towards the nearest horizons (brought absurdly nearer by the screen of rain), my patron would discard his camera and recline in his chair with his back to the fading daylight. He knew that the storm, like all those that crossed the plains, would be brief, and that most of the clouds would have passed before night, leaving the sky clear and faintly lighted. But he would reach an arm towards me and speak as though the plains as he knew them were lost to sight forever.

'This head,' he had once murmured. 'This subject of so many portraits—scrutinise it, but not for anything suggested by the oddities of its surface. No. Inspect it. Search it to disprove the worst theories of these false plainsmen around us. You have always credited them with too much subtlety. You suppose that because they have spent lives on the plains they are privy to signs you are still searching for. And yet the most perceptive of them—those you might almost have taken for visionaries—have never asked precisely where their plains are.

'I grant you that to see even those plains we revelled in all afternoon—even that is some kind of distinction. But don't be deceived. Nothing that we saw today exists apart from the darkness.

'Look. My eyes are closed. I am about to sleep. When you see me insensible, trepan me. Carve my skull neatly open. No blade can trouble me after all this alcohol. Peer into the pale brain you find pulsating there. Prise apart its dull-coloured lobes. Examine them with powerful lenses. You'll see nothing to suggest plains. They disappeared long ago—the lands I claimed to see.

'The Great Darkness. Isn't that where all our plains lie? But they're safe, quite safe. And on their far side—too far away for you and me to visit—over there the weather is changing. The skies above us all are growing lighter. Another plain altogether is drifting towards our own. We're travelling somewhere in a world the shape of an eye. And we still haven't seen what other countries that eye looks out on.'

The man always ended his speeches abruptly. I would sit with him, drinking, and listening for more. But my patron would keep his eyes closed and only ask to be kept upright after he lost consciousness.

Earlier in the day, the man used his camera as though he looked for no more than the imprint on film of a certain darkening afternoon. But I, and perhaps a few of the others, knew that our host never intended his photographs to register what anyone present might have wanted to recall of their scene.

The party always settled by the sheltered bank of a stream. During the afternoon they stationed themselves in separate groups at places overlooking the water. Even the couples who strolled some distance from the main gathering were never out of sight of the clustered trees and the greener grass beside the stream. Yet no one was ever posed against any view of pools or stony shallows. Looking at the photographs weeks later, I found no recognisable landmarks in their back-grounds. A stranger might have supposed they showed any of a dozen places miles apart.

And the people depicted were seldom as they would have remembered themselves on a given afternoon. A man who for much of the day had engaged with a young woman in some of the protracted rituals that comprised a courtship on the plains—such a man might see afterwards an image of himself conspicuous-ly alone, with his gaze drawn towards a distant group of women and even the one he had never approached.

There was no gross falsification of the events of a day. But all the collections of prints seemed meant to confuse, if not the few people who asked to 'look at themselves' afterwards, then perhaps the people who might come across the photographs years later, in their search for the earliest evidence that certain lives would proceed as they had in fact proceeded.

If any such people turned the pages of the unadorned albums where the prints had been hastily mounted, they might see eyes averted from what should have attracted them, even so long ago; a certain man anxious not to be considered one of the only group that would ever include him; another man huddled with those he would claim long afterwards never to have approached. As for the settings of those unlikely events—so few would seem part of any landscape preferred in earlier years that students of such matters might at least respect the strangeness of what was perceived in the past if they did not conclude that certain favoured sites on the plains had long since disappeared.

I often wondered myself what might be supposed years later of the scant signs of my own presence at those scenes. There were afternoons when I watched little else but the passage of changing moods across the face of my patron's eldest grand-daughter while she listened politely to the chatter of her friends and yet watched little else but the passage of breezes and shadows of clouds across the middle distance of the plain. But her grandfather always motioned me towards some group of women known as the subjects of famous portraits or as models for certain characters in fiction but apparently unaware, for the moment, of any change worth observing in the plains about them. I looked wherever my patron pointed, or I contrived with the women to seem wholly occupied with some wordless conversation or some unspoken secret and so became one of those little groups whose appearance might trouble anyone speculating in later years about such conversations and such secrets.

I and my companions of the moment got no lasting assurance from those few hours of threatened sunlight at those unremarkable places on the plains. Yet we put aside for a little while our puzzlement and uncertainty and conspired, some of us perhaps unwittingly, to seem in possession of a secret that resolved the mystery of those hours and that place at least. And in the eyes of people I would never know, my seeming

hold on something became one more cause for puzzlement and uncertainty among those people of years to
come.

What could those people do but doubt even
further their own grasp of things when they saw in some
faded, ill-arranged photograph such signs that once, at
a spot on the plains that could never be precisely identified, an oddly assorted group of people, never
renowned for their insight into such matters, had shared
a certainty, had whispered and smiled together over a
discovery, or had even stared and pointed towards a sign
that contented them for the time?

It was not only groups of people who were posed
as though within reach of one more of those certainties that anyone viewing them must lack. Many a man or
woman who would readily have confessed to seeing
nowhere but in old illustrations the weather or the
landscape that persuaded them to look for no further
skies or lands—many such had been photographed as
though whatever they looked at just out of range of the
camera yielded the sort of satisfaction that people long

afterwards could only derive from old photographs.

Some of the people who were posed in this way agreed to make some uncharacteristic gesture or to feign interest in what rarely attracted them. Others obliged the photographer by appearing as only rumour or raillery would have them. I myself had grown used to my patron's thrusting an empty camera into my hand and urging me to stand as though aiming it at some figure or landscape in the middle distance.

*

Few of the crowds at those scenes would have recalled that my original appointment to the household had been as a writer of material suitable for filmscripts. Even fewer attended the annual revelations, as they were called, when I was expected to display or describe the best of my recent projects.

It was so long since I myself had attended any such function arranged for another client of the house that I could not say whether mine had become the smallest of those gatherings. Those who did attend my own seemed not to care that empty spaces surrounded them in the reception room or that their voices, when they strolled out onto the long verandah, were overwhelmed by the din of crickets and frogs. In the first hours of the ceremony, between sunset and midnight, they huddled together as they ate and drank, and assumed the bearing of a privileged and discriminating elite: a little band who had not forgotten the retiring scholar from the rear rooms of the library and who might one day boast that they had sat through the first of his by then almost legendary revelations. At midnight, when the revelation proper began—when the women were farewelled and the traditional high-backed uncomfortable chairs were drawn up to the semicircle of tables densely set with decanters and stained at close intervals by the passage of light through massive cuboids of whisky enclosed in thicknesses of crystal—then the audience seemed more eager than mere politeness demanded. They waited expectantly while the servants locked the doors and drew together the double layers of violet drapes hung for the occasion and then mounted their ladders to seal the gaps between curtains and walls with the rolls of revelation-paper that gave off their unfailingly evocative crackling sound.

I believed I had sometimes come near to fulfilling their expectations. I had kept them listening until even a man among them who had violated the spirit of the ceremony and hidden a watch in his pocket—even that man would have been pleasantly surprised when he glanced for the last time furtively at his timepiece. And when I tugged unobserved at the bell-pull and the servants crept into the room from the distant alcove where the muffled signal had reached them, and pulled back with startling suddenness the massive drapes, I had always found some reassurance in the mild cry that went up from my hearers. Watching them stumble towards the windows, dazzled by the unexpected intensity of the light, and perhaps genuinely surprised by the view of lawn and parkland receding towards a segment of plain, I knew I had effected a revelation of some sort. But I knew, too, that I had not achieved what was so clearly described in the literature that had given rise to the ceremony.

My failing was that I could never arrange my subject matter—the arguments and narratives and expositions that kept me talking for never less than half a day—so that it culminated in a revelation that somehow emphasised or contrasted with or prefigured or even seemed to deny all likelihood of the lesser revelation of the land outside appearing suddenly in an unexpected light. I could not complain that I lacked the advantages of other salaried clients—the dramatists, toymakers, weavers, illusionists, curators of indoor gardens, musicians, metalworkers, keepers of aviaries and aquaria, poets, puppeteers, singers and reciters, designers and modellers of impractical costumes, historians of horseracing, clowns, collectors of mandalas and mantras, inventors of inconclusive board-games, and others who could use so much more than mere words to produce their effects. For I myself, in my first years at that house, had been provided with enough equipment to prepare and display any film that I might have devised. It was my own decision to stand before the spectators at my earliest revelations with only a blank screen behind me and an empty projector pointing at me from a corner of the partly darkened room and to talk for sixteen hours of landscapes that only I could interpret. I had thought then that one or two of my listeners, when the curtains were dragged back to reveal a land in the depths of an afternoon whose beginnings none of them had witnessed, saw in the plain before them a place they had always hoped to explore. But in later years, when I stood before my dwindling audience, still in a darkened room but with not even the blank screen to suggest that the landscapes and figures I argued for might soon be represented by scenes and people drawn from their own country, then I suspected that even my most attentive listeners took as their revelation only the appearance once more of the plains that my hours of speculative talk had made to seem just a little more promising.

There were occasions throughout each year when I wondered why my following had not lapsed entirely.

Even in the inmost rooms of the library, on the third storey of the north-east wing, I sometimes heard, across courtyards shaded from the late afternoon sunlight or swept by the flight of bats at dusk, the first, and then, after an interval almost exactly predictable, the second of the immoderate roars that marked the dual climax of some revelation by a client whose final achievement had been to suggest, through the difficult medium of his particular craft, some detail of a plain paradoxically apart from, and yet defining further, the land revealed moments afterwards between the ponderously parting curtains.

There were so many clients with their studios and workshops in the several wings reserved for them, or even in the tree-shaded lodges in the parks between the furthest lawns and the nearest of the forested hills, that I heard almost weekly those cries of admiration for still another statement of the endlessly variable theme of plains returning, enhanced but still recognisable, to view. Even the most eager of the scholars and bene-factors in those audiences had to forgo many a performance. I expected each year, when my own fell due again, to find that the whole household had retired early after some taxing day and night of drinking and watching, that not a single car had arrived from the neighbouring estates, and that I would have to emulate those few clients I sometimes heard of who emerged each year from their quiet quarters and presented their revelations in front of empty rooms and stoppered decanters. I had often anticipated the moment when the servants, with every show of decorum, drew back the curtains so that the presence of the plains filled the silent room while I myself tried to see them from the position that was the ideal centre of my absent audience. But each year a few remained of my previous year's following, and a few others had arrived to hear me out, perhaps even preferring me to some celebrated client whose approaching revelation was already being talked about at the very table where I presided in silence over the whisky.

The reason for this lingering interest in me may have been nothing more than the common preference of plainsfolk for the concealed rather than the obvious—their weakness for expecting much from the unfavoured or the little-known. Although I asked no questions on my own behalf, I learned in time that I was considered by a small group to be a film-maker of exceptional promise. When I first heard this, I had been about to reply that my cabinets full of notes and preliminary drafts would probably never give rise to any image of any sort of plain. I had almost decided to call myself poet or novelist or landscaper or memorialist or scene-setter or some other of the many sorts of literary practitioner flourishing on the plains. Yet if I had announced such a change in my profession I might have lost the support of those few people who persisted in esteeming me. For although writing was generally considered by plainsmen the worthiest of all crafts and the one most nearly able to resolve the thousand uncertainties that hung about almost every mile of the plains, still, if I had claimed even a small part of the tribute paid to writers I would probably have fallen out of favour with even those who shared this view of prose and verse. For my most sincere admirers were aware also of the plainsman's scant interest in films and of the often-heard claim that a camera merely multiplied the least significant qualities of the plains—their colour and shape as they appeared to the eye. These followers of mine almost certainly shared in this mistrust of the uses of film, for they never suggested to me that I might one day devise scenes that no one could have predicted. What they praised was my apparent reluctance to work with camera or projector and my years spent in writing and rewriting notes for introducing to a conjectured audience images still unseen. A few of these men argued even that the further my researches took me away from my announced aim and the less my notes seemed likely to result in any visible film, the more credit I deserved as the explorer of a distinctive landscape. And if this argument seemed to classify me as a writer rather than a film-maker, then my loyal followers were not perturbed. For their very denials justified their belief that I was practising the most demanding and praise-worthy of all the specialised forms of writing—that which came near to defining what was indefinable about the plains by attempting an altogether different task. It suited the purposes of these men that I should continue to call myself a film-maker; that I should sometimes appear at my annual revelation with a blank screen behind me and should talk of the images I might yet display. For these men were confident that the more I strove to depict even one distinctive landscape—one arrangement of light and surfaces to suggest a moment on some plain I was sure of—the more I would lose myself in the manifold ways of words with no known plains behind them.

In the years when my work was most often interrupted by my patron's fondness for scenes, there might have been a handful left of those supporters who talked knowingly sometimes of the neglected film-maker preparing his great work in the seclusion of the library. They would have been the least likely of anyone at a scene to be deceived by the sight of me pointing an empty camera towards some everyday sight. Perhaps they felt obliged to make some comment on the irrelevance of such things as lenses and light waves to the creation of those images of mine that no one had yet laid eyes on. But usually they joined unnoticed in the general amusement to see, posed as one eager to record the play of light at some moment of an uneventful afternoon, the very man who allowed whole seasons to pass while he sat behind drawn blinds in the least-visited rooms of a silent library.

I seldom wondered what opinion of me predominated among the people who watched and smiled as I took my awkward grip on some antiquated camera and stared obligingly at some empty zone ahead of me. I was far more concerned with those who might one day examine the faulty prints in my patron's jumbled collection and see me as a man with my eyes fixed on something that mattered. Even the few who had heard or read of my efforts to discover a fitting landscape— even they might have supposed that I sometimes looked no further than my surroundings. No one afterwards could point to a single feature of whatever place I stared at. It was still a place out of sight in a scene arranged by someone who was himself out of sight. But anyone might have decided that I recognised the meaning of what I saw.

And so, on those darkening afternoons, at those scenes whose scenery seemed more often pointed at than observed, whenever the camera in my hand put me in mind of some young woman who might see me years afterwards as a man who saw further than others, I would always ask my patron at last to record the moment when I lifted my own camera to my face and stood with my eye pressed against the lens and my finger poised as if to expose to the film in its dark chamber the darkness that was the only visible sign of whatever I saw beyond myself.